Whacked in the Woods

WREN AND RASCAL COZY MYSTERY, BOOK 2

JUDITH A. BARRETT

Wobbly Creek

WOBBLY CREEK, LLC

Whacked in the Woods

Wren and Rascal Cozy Mystery, Book 2

Published in the United States of America by Wobbly Creek, LLC

2023 Georgia

wobblycreek.com

Cover by Wobbly Creek, LLC

ISBN 978-1-953870-43-8 ebook

ISBN 978-1-953870-44-5 paperback

DEDICATION

Whacked in the Woods is dedicated to the colors green and yellow, to old and new friends, and especially to dogs.

ALSO BY JUDITH A. BARRETT

Riley Malloy Mystery Series

Maggie Sloan Thriller Series

Grid Down Survival Series

Donut Lady Cozy Mystery Series

Wren and Rascal Cozy Mystery Series

Previously

WREN

My name is Wren Weaver; I'm a freelance journalist and a camping enthusiast which is why I accepted an assignment with a travel magazine to write four articles about haunted campgrounds across the United States and to provide feedback for the manufacturer's camping trailers. I don't write fiction; I don't mean to sound snobby: it's just not my niche.

Rascal, my four-year-old, sweet, black and tan, mostly Labrador Retriever with a smidgeon of Husky, and I began our first assignment in Hidden Gulch, Arizona, at the Forgotten Oasis Campground.

Rascal and I felt like we'd found our home at Hidden Gulch. We were there only a week, but Socorro, the owner of the campground, and Betsy, the campground office manager, became our close friends along with Thomas, the frequently annoying ghost of the Forgotten Oasis.

The person I will miss most of all is the county marshal, Justin Lewis. I was really torn because I could have stayed in Hidden Gulch to see if our budding friendship would become something more interesting, except I have never quit before a project was done, and I have three more articles to write. I don't know how strong the relationship is between Justin and me; I'll be heartbroken if it falls apart before it's had a chance to grow.

My publisher, Charlie Hogue, tried to play both sides of the fence when he hired a new editor; the editor thought he had the right to rewrite my article that was based on local lore and replace it with a poorly written, confusing story with the editor's idea of a more suitable ghost than the saloon lady.

After I delivered an ultimatum: my article as written, or the editor can take over the remaining assignments, Charlie reluctantly decided to publish my article. I think Justin was a little disappointed, which is kind of sweet now that I think about it.

Charlie and his editor were a minor annoyance, though, in comparison to the killer who attacked my friends: the librarian then Socorro and left both of them for dead.

After I stopped the killer before he murdered Socorro's brother-in-law and me, Rascal and I left Hidden Gulch, but not before I left Marshal Justin Lewis with a kiss he couldn't forget.

Rascal and I will arrive at Lonesome Trail Campground in Dry Creek, Texas, later today, for our second assignment. I'm going to see if I can write the article in less time than it took me in Hidden Gulch.

JUSTIN

I came to Hidden Gulch three years ago as a favor to my dad. The marshal at Hidden Gulch was an old friend of Dad's and had been trying to find a replacement for two years, so he could retire. I agreed to take over temporarily until the town found a permanent replacement. I discovered the slow pace of a small town was what I needed to begin healing after I lost my wife in a car crash, so I stayed.

When Wren and Rascal came into town, my quiet, orderly life turned upside down. I thought I was immune to women, but Wren blasted that notion right out of my head the first time I saw her. When she spoke to me in her soft, Georgia accent, my heart that I thought had been frozen in time, melted. She's petite and looks so fragile, but that green-eyed beauty with light brown hair with its streaks of red that look like fire is absolutely fearless, and she terrifies me with the chances she takes.

If I'd had my way, she would have stayed in Hidden Gulch, but she promised Thomas she'd be back in six weeks; judging by that last kiss we shared, I'm hopeful she'll be here permanently.

Chapter One

When Wren turned at the faded sign, Lonesome Trail Campground, she stopped in the middle of the gravel road with overgrown weeds along the sides that threatened to take over the road and peered ahead.

"Can this be right, Rascal? I almost didn't see the sign because it was hidden in the brush and the trees alongside the road. I hope there's another road for the exit because it looks like it's one lane."

Wren crept along as she tried to avoid the deep ruts. "The fences along the county road, the sign, and the entrance are suffering from neglect, and this road isn't any better. I'm fine with a haunted campground, but this looks like an abandoned campground."

After she reached a clearing, she scanned the area; she raised her eyebrows at the large, dilapidated wooden building with a rusty, metal roof and a small, faded sign on the door that said, "Registration." The building was surrounded by dirt with small patches of grass.

Wren scanned the campground sites and wrinkled her nose. "Doesn't look very inviting, does it, Rascal? I hope we get a site that's relatively level. I don't see any sites with a concrete slab or even gravel, and some of the picnic tables look like they'd collapse if you put a cup of coffee on them."

She drove slowly to the office. "Everything is suffering from delayed maintenance. The good news is there has to be a story, right?"

Rascal yipped.

After she parked in front of the office, she opened the pickup door to the backseat, so Rascal could hop out.

"Are you going to wait outside?" Wren asked as she stepped up on the small porch. Rascal trotted to the door.

"Let's go in." Wren turned the doorknob, but it didn't turn, so she leaned against it and pushed, and the door flew open.

She shook her head. *What is it with me and doors?*

An elderly woman whose frail, brown skin was so thin that it had a translucent cast to it sat on a stool at the registration desk with her back to the door and a comic book-sized booklet in front of her. She was hunched over the booklet with her face only inches from the page.

She turned, and her dark eyes widened as Wren caught herself from falling by grabbing onto the doorknob.

The old woman sat up straight as she shook her head. "I was working on my crossword puzzle. I sit on this side of the desk, so it's clear that I do my crosswords only on my break and never on company time."

She slid off the stool then peered at Wren through her thick glasses as she closed her booklet with her pencil remaining in the crease to save her page.

She scurried to the other side of the desk. "You must be Wren Weaver; actually, you don't have to be Wren Weaver if you don't care to, but it is important to be true to oneself, young lady."

I have no idea what she just said. Wren smiled. "I'm Wren Weaver; my publisher made a reservation for me for the week."

"If you're speaking of Charles Hogue, he called yesterday and paid for two weeks. He said he wanted you to take all the time you need to write your article. Are you going to write about the famous Lonesome Trail

Railroad? I have several brochures that I've saved from the days when the railroad attracted people from everywhere." The woman pointed to a brochure on the desk, and Wren picked it up.

"Thank you. Do you have anything for me to sign or a map that will show me where our site is?" Wren asked.

"All the paperwork's been taken care of. Just mosey around and pick a site for yourself, Miss Weaver, but don't pick anything in the second row because the electricity's not working in that row."

Wren furrowed her brow as she glanced at the brochure. "Is the Lonesome Trail Railroad part of the campground?"

"It was; the campground and a park with a small zoo were owned by our family until the 1940s when the heirs sold the original parcel to a land speculator. Of course, the speculator's fancy plans never materialized, so he split the property into two pieces and sold them separately. My nephew, Walt, and his son, Gage, recently bought the campground and have a priority list of improvements; I think the electrical, water, and septic systems are at the top of their list."

"Is there a problem with the utilities?" Wren asked.

"The squirrels have had free rein to the property for quite a while. Walt thinks they damaged a lot of the wiring that was supposed to be underground; guess it wasn't quite deep enough. The septic in the back row needs to be inspected; it might have been skipped a few years while the last owner was still alive; we can't find any record of any inspections in the previous ten years, so Gage has scheduled inspections for all the utilities this week. He's very thorough, Miss Weaver."

"Please call me Wren." Wren smiled.

The woman glanced around; Wren did the same.

"Are you expecting someone?" Wren asked.

"You never know around here, Wren. I'm Jenna Lee Navarro. You may call me Miss Jenna Lee. I've never been married and don't plan to be any time soon. Why don't you look on the third row at the second site from the restrooms and laundry? It's my personal favorite."

"Thank you, Miss Jenna Lee. Is there a grocery store nearby?" Wren asked.

"The closest grocery store is thirty miles east of here. You can't miss it because after you pass our local gas station, there's nothing between here and there except wildlife and beautiful, old live oak trees. If you're not looking to spend that much time on the road after your long drive from Arizona, our gas station is only a mile up the road and is fairly well stocked with vittles; you might want to stop there first. The diner across the road from it serves breakfast and lunch; they're open from six in the morning until three in the afternoon, so you have options to keep you from starving." The old woman tittered.

As Wren and Rascal headed toward the door, Miss Jenna Lee said, "I didn't catch his name."

Whose name?

When Wren turned to ask, she smiled as Miss Jenna Lee pointed to Rascal. "This is Rascal; I apologize, I should have introduced him."

Miss Jenna Lee nodded. "It's a pleasure to make your acquaintance, Rascal."

Rascal grinned as Miss Jenna Lee stepped out from behind the desk and stood in front of him with her fist close to her chest.

Rascal immediately sat for whatever she had in her hand.

Miss Jenna Lee giggled then held out the dog treat.

When Rascal gently took it from her hand, Miss Jenna Lee cooed as she rubbed his face with both hands, "You are such a good boy."

After Wren and Rascal were in the pickup, Wren said, "Miss Jenna Lee might be a little confusing to listen to, but anyone who keeps dog treats at their desk is a great person."

Rascal yipped.

Wren found the site that Miss Jenna Lee said was her favorite. She was close to the building that housed the laundry and the restrooms, and just a few steps away from the women's restroom. After she parked, she scanned their site as she and Rascal climbed out of the truck.

"Our site is level and shady, and we have a picnic table that's in great shape. There's no grass, but we'll put down our large outdoor mat like we used at the Forgotten Oasis. This is definitely the prime site here."

After she plugged into the electrical outlet, hooked the hose to the water faucet and turned it on, and secured the sewer hose to its connection, Wren and Rascal went inside the camper. Wren turned on the air conditioner and adjusted it to cool down their tiny trailer.

"We'll probably let it run all night." Wren sighed. "I wish the camper had a thermostat for the air conditioner like it does for the heater. It's really annoying to have to turn it on and off manually. At least I got a nice blanket when we went through Abilene, so I won't freeze again in the middle of the night when the temperature drops. So far, the camper is not much of an improvement over the one we had in Arizona, and this campground is nothing like Forgotten Oasis, is it?"

Wren sighed. "I sound homesick for Arizona, don't I?"

She pulled out a bottle of water from the refrigerator and sat at one end of the U-shaped bench that hugged the oversized dining table that was laughingly called a dinette even though its length was only a few inches shy of the tiny camper's width.

She read the brochure Miss Jenna Lee had given her. "Evidently, the Lonesome Trail Railroad had a miniature train with open passenger cars that circled a small zoo then traveled through a large park with several small villages alongside the tracks. Let's ask Miss Jenna Lee if it's okay for us to go exploring; maybe there's a path somewhere."

Wren turned over the brochure. "The date this was printed has faded; it must have been a long time ago. I'll bet it was an exciting place to visit in its heyday."

Wren's phone rang, and she grinned as she answered.

"Is this a bad time to call?" Justin asked.

"Not at all; Rascal and I are at the Lonesome Trail Campground, and I just finished setting up. What are you doing?"

"I'm in my office for a late lunch break and thought I'd check in with you. How was your drive today?"

"There was very little traffic because I decided to take the back roads. Rascal napped most of the way, and I enjoyed the scenery."

"Let's plan a road trip for the three of us after your assignment is over. Where would you like to go?"

"Back to Arizona," Wren said.

"That's my girl, so I guess my break's over because someone's at my door."

After he hung up, Wren sighed. "Let's get some fuel and see what we can find at the gas station in the way of something for supper."

When Wren drove past the office, a sign on the door directed any late arrivals to pick a site and stop by the office in the morning to pay.

"Miss Jenna Lee must have waited for us because this says the office hours are until two; that was nice of her, wasn't it? We'll talk to her in the morning about the Lonesome Trail Railroad."

Wren smiled at the large, rectangular, metal sign alongside the road; its edges had rusted, and the once-red background had faded to a soft brown. The black lettering had weathered but the name was still readable: "Dry

Creek Gas & Grub." A plume of smoke coming from behind the gas station drifted across the parking lot and toward the road in a lazy dance.

When Wren opened her door to fill the tank, she inhaled the tantalizing aroma of smoking meat; Rascal whined.

"It does smell amazing, doesn't it?"

After she filled the pickup's tank, Wren parked near the entrance to the store in the shade. "I'll leave the windows open for you, Rascal. Today is humid and warm, but it's still not the scorching heat of Arizona, and there's a nice breeze."

When she went inside, the heady bouquet of smoked beef swirled throughout the store. Wren hurried to the back and stood in line for the window marked "Order Here".

She peered around the tall man in front of her who wore cowboy boots and a large, brimmed cowboy hat. She furrowed her brow as she stared at the prominent blackboard on the wall behind the cash register with its menu hand-printed with chalk.

"Do I want a small or medium order?" she muttered.

The young man in front of her turned and smiled. "Didn't mean to eavesdrop, ma'am, but I noticed your dog in your truck. You might want to get a medium if you plan on sharing with your companion."

Wren returned his smile. "Thank you; I'm used to talking to Rascal, and sometimes I forget he's not standing right next to me."

"I'm happy I could fill in for that handsome fella. Is he a lab and husky mix?"

"That's exactly what he is, at least according to our vet; you've got a good eye."

The young man chuckled. "I pay more attention to dogs than people; they're much more interesting. I'm Gage." He held out his hand.

"Wren."

After they shook hands, Gage said, "You must be the journalist Aunt Jenna Lee was expecting this afternoon; she said you're writing about the campground."

"I'm on assignment for a travel magazine to write articles about haunted campgrounds."

"Is that what you were doing in Arizona?" Gage chuckled. "There are few secrets when it comes to Aunt Jenna Lee."

Good to know. Wren nodded. "Is there a story about the Lonesome Trail Campground being haunted?"

"There is; Aunt Jenna Lee would be delighted if you ask her. It's actually a very tragic story, which Aunt Jenna Lee tells much more dramatically than I ever could. Take a coffee cup with you when you go to the office, and she'll refill it with a special blend of coffee she orders from San Antonio."

"Are you staying at the campground?" Wren asked.

"My great-great-great-uncle built a small house on the grounds. I'm not sure how many greats, so I always say three because that's what Aunt Jenna Lee says. I figure people get the idea." Gage smiled. "You may not have noticed it because it's well-hidden in the trees. Would it be too forward if I invite myself to your site for dessert, if I bring the dessert? I've always enjoyed the sunsets at the campground, but after the sun goes down, the mosquitos come out in force, so I definitely won't be wearing out my welcome."

Wren smiled. "I'd enjoy the company, and I would never turn down dessert."

When it was his turn to order, Gage said, "Go ahead, Wren; be sure to ask for burnt ends. I'll see you in a bit."

"Medium brisket with burnt ends, and a small coleslaw," Wren said.

"Yes, ma'am; good choice, Miss Weaver." The young woman smiled.

"Small town; news gets around fast," Gage whispered.

Wren nodded. *No surprise. I need to research burnt ends.*

When Wren carried her food out of the building, she glanced across the street. The diner's sign was the full length of an old train dining car; the words "Whistle Stop Diner" stretched boldly across the sign with a smiling steam locomotive that sported a chef's hat in place of the smokestack in the upper left corner; a steaming cup of coffee and a piece of pie topped by a generous dollop of ice cream that threatened to drip onto its plate were on the upper right corner.

After Wren joined Rascal in the pickup, she said, "I'll have to take a picture of the diner for Betsy. She'll love it."

Rascal leaned over the seat to get a closer whiff of the contents of the large white sack that Wren had set on the passenger's seat.

Wren chuckled. "I got enough for you. I'll mix it with your food for a Texas treat."

She headed toward the campground. "I met the owner of the Lonesome Trail Campground; his name is Gage, and he seems like a nice guy. He'll come to our site later with dessert and to watch the sunset. I'll be interested in his strategy for revitalizing the campground."

Rascal softly growled.

"Don't be such a worry wart. I'm not going to grill him: I'll just politely inquire."

Wren glanced in her rearview mirror as Rascal grinned.

"You are such a fussbudget sometimes, Rascal," she grumbled.

After they returned to the camper, Wren examined the brisket and picked out a dark piece and popped it into her mouth.

"Yum; it's crunchy, sweet, and smoky." She fished out another piece. "Also, addictive."

Wren ate two more pieces before Rascal whined. She added a spoonful of brisket to Rascal's food bowl and mixed it with his regular food. While he ate, she put a generous serving on her plate then added a small serving of coleslaw.

Rascal gobbled down his supper long before Wren had completed serving herself. She poured a large glass of sweet tea then sat at the oversized dinette to enjoy her scrumptious meal.

Mmmm; really good, and I have leftovers for tomorrow night.

After she washed her dishes and put away her leftovers, Wren set up her computer and logged into the campground wi-fi to search for more information about the Lonesome Trail Railroad; she watched the spinning circle on her screen until her search timed out.

That's not good. I'll ask Miss Jenna Lee about the wi-fi tomorrow morning in case it's a glitch. If she tells me that's the best it gets, I'll mention it to Gage.

As she pulled out her phone to set it up for wi-fi, Rascal whined; she put away her phone and opened the door.

Gage smiled. "Did Rascal tell you I was here?"

Rascal wagged then followed Wren as she stepped out of the camper.

"Don't see many awnings on small trailers." Gage leaned to scratch Rascal's ear. "I grabbed a tablecloth from the store in case you don't have one."

Gage spread out the vinyl tablecloth then set the large, brown paper grocery sack on the table. "Have you ever had fresh-squeezed lemonade? I came across a food truck between here and San Antonio, where I live, so I picked up a couple of quarts on my way here this morning. The gas station bakes fresh cookies three times a day, so they're better than homemade because they take care of the kitchen clean-up."

Wren smiled. "I don't think I've ever had any kind of lemonade except frozen; no way could I pass up lemonade from a food truck and gas station cookies."

Gage opened a quart of lemonade before he put the small, white sack of cookies on the table and pulled out the napkins and cups that were in the sack.

After they each had two cookies on a napkin in front of them, Gage lifted his glass. "Salud."

Wren smiled and copied him. "Salud."

Wren sipped her lemonade then took a bite of the still-warm chocolate chip cookie. "This is good."

Gage nodded. "My favorite. So, tell me more about your assignment."

"The publisher hired me to write articles about four haunted campgrounds. Lonesome Trail is my second campground. The RV manufacturer is providing campers for me to use, and I'm providing feedback of the pros and cons of each trailer to my publisher, who sends my comments to the CEO."

"Aunt Jenna Lee said you'll be here for two weeks."

"I have two weeks to write my article; I wrote my first article in a week, so we'll see. Tell me about your plans for the campground."

"My dad and I are partners. Our priority is to complete an assessment of the basics for the campground; we'd like to expand the campground sites, add another building for restrooms, and enlarge and renovate the office to include a camp store. After the campground is updated, Dad hopes to turn the old Lonesome Trail Railroad Zoo into a donkey rescue park with walking trails that wind past the villages, which means recreating the old villages from the few old black and white photos we have."

"Sounds very ambitious." Wren polished off her cookie and sipped on her lemonade.

"That's what Mom says, but after Dad retired, he decided he needed something to keep him busy, and I was getting bored in the corporate world."

"What did you do?"

"I was the vice president of marketing for a major retailer; I've always loved marketing, but the day-to-day operations that kept the department running smoothly became too routine for me. When Dad talked about doing something with our property here, his excitement was contagious." Gage chuckled. "Mom must have natural immunity because she thinks we're nuts. What about your folks? Are they worried about you traveling by yourself?"

Rascal whined.

"Excuse me, Rascal," Gage said. "I meant to say Wren and you traveling by yourselves."

A brief smile curved Wren's lips. "Rascal is a sensitive guy, Gage. I can't imagine why my parents would worry; I've always loved writing, and my first memory of camping with my parents was when I was two. My grandmother told my mom that I was a feral child because I was raised in a tent. Grandma definitely didn't share my parents' vision and enthusiasm for outdoor recreation."

Gage nodded. "I think you nailed it: Mom doesn't share our vision of the possibilities here." Gage pointed toward the west. "Just look at that sunset; money can't buy that."

Wren gazed at the western sky as the colors over the trees shifted from pale yellow to orange then red; when the last light from the sinking sun burst into a brilliance of red with dancing fingers of gold, Wren gasped. "It looks like the trees are on fire."

"Takes your breath away, doesn't it?" Gage smacked his arm. "And that's our cue to call it a night."

Gage picked up their empty glasses and napkins. "I enjoyed meeting you, Wren. Let Aunt Jenna Lee know if you need anything. She has her moments, but that's just how she is these days."

Wren smiled. "Thanks. Ready to go inside, Rascal?"

Rascal dashed to the door, and they hurried inside before the onslaught of mosquitos followed them.

Wren sat at her dinette with a spiral notebook and a pen to take notes about the campground, the area, and the Lonesome Trail Railroad. As she sketched out a plan for her article, her phone rang.

"Hey, Texas Gal; how y'all doing?" Betsy asked in her best impression of a Texas drawl.

Wren snickered. "It's been a typical day: you know, stompin' snakes and wrasslin' bears."

Betsy chuckled. "Boring life of a writer. We had some excitement in Hidden Gulch. One of the most popular teachers in school gave notice; her husband, who has worked at a bank in Phoenix for five years, has been transferred to Charlotte, North Carolina, and she's going with him. Can you imagine that? The school board is in a tizzy."

"That's a real blow to the school, isn't it?"

"Sure is; the good news is that she's willing to stay until the end of next month; if the school can find the right replacement or even a temporary teacher for the rest of the year, the transition will be smoother for the children. Two members of the school board called me today and asked me to apply; that was a definite no for me. I like gazing at numbers that are neatly lined up and harmoniously balanced; in my limited experience, kiddos are neither."

Wren smiled. "You painted a clear picture of your lack of qualifications and interests in teaching; you are definitely a natural born bean counter."

"Don't let the word get out. How's my Rascal?"

"He moped the first two days; I don't blame him because I miss Hidden Gulch too, but we're mildly settled in. I haven't heard the story of why the campground is haunted yet."

"Since it's not haunted, send old Charlie an email with the subject, The End, and come back," Betsy said.

Wren chuckled. "You're a terrible influence."

"And proud of it too." Betsy sighed. "If you aren't packing up to come right back, hurry up and write something, so I can scoff at the non-haunted campground."

After they hung up, Wren smiled as she stroked Rascal's neck. "I always feel better after I talk to Betsy."

Wren jotted down a few more notes about the weather and the trees then added a little about the sunset and mosquitoes. After she rose to stretch, Wren glanced at her phone. *It's almost nine thirty. Justin will be calling soon.*

When her phone rang, Wren's eyes widened. *Mom? It's almost ten thirty in Georgia.*

"Hi, Mom. Is everything okay?"

"Dad's fine; I'm fine, but Charlie is a mess. He called me to complain that you're too harsh on his fragile editor. He has no concept of time, does he? Anyway, he wanted me to tell you to be a little more delicate when you send feedback, so I thought I'd let you know that I think you should double-down. From what Charlie sniveled about, I think you're doing great with an absolutely spineless publisher and a whiny, self-centered editor. I know Blake was your best friend in college, but I thought he was a bit self-absorbed too. What is it with these young men and their pompous attitudes? So, how's Rascal?"

Wren laughed. "Mom, you're the best. Rascal's fine; both of us were a little mopey the first two days after we left Hidden Gulch, but we're okay now. I hope to get filled in tomorrow on why this campground has been called haunted."

"Keep me posted and let me know when I can pull out my flamethrower and blast Charlie. Love you."

"Love you too, Mom."

After they hung up, Wren smiled as she resumed writing notes. "Charlie better watch it, Rascal; he's irritated Mom." She shook her head. "Mom mentioned Blake; just the thought of him makes me shudder. I was crushed when he dumped me for that shallow, ambitious blonde, but in retrospect, she did me a favor because I finally saw him for the self-centered jerk that he was."

Wren glanced at her phone. "It's ten o'clock; I expected to hear from Justin by now. Want to take a last break, Rascal?"

Wren took her phone with her while she and Rascal were outside. When her phone buzzed a text, she exhaled in relief as she read it. "Sorry, honey. Stuck in a meeting."

She replied, "Call after the meeting; I'm working on an outline for the Texas article, so I'll be up late."

"Will do. Thanks."

"Ready to go back inside and stay awake a while, Rascal? I have a few ideas on different approaches for my research while we wait to hear from Justin."

Wren read about unincorporated towns in Texas, census records for the county, and school districts then followed a thread that led to an Oklahoma City newspaper article written in the mid-1920s about a young girl who drowned in a moat at a small zoo. The article continued with statistics about drownings, safety precautions to prevent drownings, and a list of boat safety courses.

"That didn't help," Wren grumbled.

She furrowed her brow then narrowed her eyes as she bent over her keyboard. "I have an idea."

When Wren's phone rang, Rascal yipped.

"Thanks, Rascal; I was heads-down and didn't hear it."

Wren smiled as she answered. "Hey, Marshal. Who corralled you into a late-night meeting?"

Justin exhaled. "The school board; have you talked to Betsy?"

"Yes, she told me about the teacher leaving."

"The school board decided they needed more people to be involved in the process of hiring a teacher. I don't know exactly how I ended up getting the short stick, but I did. The state school board association is advising our school district on best practices for advertising for teachers. I'm on the small team of second tier screeners."

"How small?" Wren asked.

"Just me, so far. I need to get a couple other people to join me. Do you think I'd be able to entice Betsy?"

"Tell her she won't be eligible for the position if she's on the screening team; she'll jump on it."

Justin chuckled. "Thanks; that's a perfect pitch. Got any more ideas?"

"Go to the coffee shop; there are a couple of the older ladies that I've seen there that are ultra-sharp. You'll know who to ask if you sit with a cup of coffee because there's one in particular, and I'm sorry I don't know her name, but she'll casually ask you how I'm doing."

"I think I know who you mean; that's a great idea. Did you know you have remarkable observation skills?"

"Sometimes I know that, but most of the time, I think I'm a dud."

Justin snorted. "You are far from being a dud. Since I've drafted you as my advisor, what about another man on the team, so I'm not outnumbered?"

"Ask the lady from the coffee shop who she would suggest." Wren unsuccessfully tried to hold back a yawn. "'Scuse me."

"Brilliant as usual; it's late there, and you've had a long day. I'll call tomorrow, hopefully at our usual time. Good night."

"Sweet dreams."

Chapter Two

Rascal whined; Wren opened her eyes. "It's barely daylight; what time is it?" She glanced at her phone. "Six o'clock. It's not terrible, but it would have been nice to sleep another hour or two."

Wren groaned as she rolled out of bed and stumbled to her coffeemaker to push the button. "Thank goodness I had sense enough to set it up before I went to bed."

While the coffeemaker gurgled and sputtered, Wren brushed her hair then poured the steaming coffee into her largest cup and stepped into her boots before she and Rascal went outside for his first break of the morning.

Wren yawned as she sat at her picnic table; while she sipped her coffee, she glanced down and snorted. *I'm wearing my baby duck pajamas with the capri length bottoms and my western boots with no socks. Am I a fashionista or what?*

Rascal explored the area around their site and the vacant site next to them. Wren glanced behind her when she heard the crunch of tires and sighed.

I didn't expect anyone else to be up this early.

"Good morning, Gage."

"Hey, Wren. You and Rascal are up early; Aunt Jenna Lee invited me to take her to breakfast at the Whistle Stop. Care to join us? I'm supposed to pick her up in a half hour. We'll swing by for you right after that."

"That sounds great." Wren forced herself to stay seated, even though she wanted to jump up and run inside. *Maybe he hasn't noticed my baby duck pajamas.*

"See you in a bit; I was cruising the property before Dad arrived." Gage waved as he sped toward the office in the golf cart.

When he rounded the corner, Wren rushed into the camper with Rascal on her heels.

After she fed Rascal then dressed, she glanced at the mirror. "At least I brushed my hair before we went outside. Are you ready for one more break?"

While Rascal did his business, Wren watched the other campground guests as they headed toward the exit in their trucks for work; most of them waved when they passed her row, and she smiled and returned their waves.

I get it; it's lonely being at the campground alone with no one to wave good-bye when they leave for work.

Her spirits lifted when her phone buzzed a text from Justin. "Good morning. I miss you."

"I miss you too." She added a smiley face before she sent the text.

He's up awfully early. I wonder if something's wrong. She sent another text. "Why are you up so early?"

"Busted. Set my alarm, so I could text you first thing."

That's the sweetest thing anyone's ever done for me. "Go back to bed. Sweet dreams."

Wren exhaled. "Gage and Miss Jenna Lee will be here any minute, Rascal; let's go inside."

Wren refilled Rascal's water bowl and grabbed her sunglasses and backpack. After she hugged Rascal, she locked the camper door as Gage pulled in at her site. She peered at his truck. *Where's Miss Jenna Lee?*

Gage climbed out of his truck and met Wren before she reached the truck. "Aunt Jenna Lee's in the back seat. She said you're the guest and must ride in the front, and she's royalty, so she must be chauffeured."

Wren giggled. "Can't say she's wrong."

Gage nodded. "She comes up with stuff like that all the time. Dad calls it Aunt Jenna Lee logic; we don't argue because we'd lose."

As they drove to the diner, Miss Jenna Lee tapped on Wren's shoulder. "What do you need to know to write your article?"

When Wren turned her head to speak, Gage winked, and she smiled. *Perfect opening.*

"According to Charlie Hogue, Lonesome Trail Campground is haunted."

Miss Jenna Lee raised her eyebrows. "Is that so, and he didn't bother to give you any details?" She snorted. "Mr. Hogue just lost all his points with me, that worthless blockhead. We'll talk after breakfast; bring Rascal to the office."

When they walked into the diner, a man who sat at the counter said, "Hey, Wren."

"How y'all doing?" she asked.

"Right as rain, girl."

Miss Jenna Lee slid into a booth with her back to the door; Wren slid in across from her, and Gage sat next to Wren. After they were seated, Miss Jenna Lee leaned across the table and whispered, "That's Humberto; he's at site number 32."

"Thank you; I figured he must be staying at the campground; I waved to everybody that waved to me when they left this morning," Wren whispered.

Gabe raised his eyebrows as he turned to face Wren. "That was really nice."

Miss Jenna Lee snorted. "Don't sound so surprised. Wren is one of the rare ones: she understands people; our guests miss their families."

A young woman with her hair braided into pigtails stopped at their booth, set down three coffee cups, and filled them from the pot of coffee that she carried.

"Coffee everyone?" she giggled as she darted to the next booth with her coffee pot.

When she reappeared with the empty pot, she asked, "Your usual, Miss Jenna Lee? What about your companions?"

"The special," Miss Jenna Lee said.

"Gotcha." The server rushed to the other end of the dining car, stopped at the order window, and shouted, "One royal, and two royal servants."

Wren giggled. "What on earth, Miss Jenna Lee?"

Miss Jenna Lee smiled. "It's our little joke: the only thing the diner serves before eight o'clock is the breakfast burrito; all these men need to get to work, so it's the breakfast burrito or wait until after eight o'clock."

"Does anyone accidently walk in and try to order something else?" Wren asked.

The old woman raised her eyebrows. "Do you see any menus? When our food is served, ask Stephanie how much a fried egg and toast is."

"This is a trap." Wren wiggled her eyebrows.

"Yes." Miss Jenna Lee's eyes crinkled as she smiled.

When Stephanie placed their burritos in front of them, Wren said, "Miss Jenna Lee told me to ask how much a fried egg and toast would be."

When Stephanie glanced around the diner, Wren bit her lip, so she wouldn't do the same.

Stephanie whispered, "Our usual price before nine o'clock is forty-seven dollars; I can knock off ten bucks for you if you can keep it quiet."

Wren laughed as Stephanie winked.

While they ate, a man came into the diner who looked exactly like Gage would look in twenty-five years.

Gage waved. "We're back here, Dad."

Stephanie called out, "I'll bring you coffee and a burrito in two shakes, Mr. Walt."

Walt kissed Miss Jenna Lee's cheek and sat next to her then extended his hand across the table. "I'm Walt, Wren; it's nice to meet you."

After they shook hands, Miss Jenna Lee said, "Wren, the original property was a zoo, the railroad station and its train tracks, and a park; Walt is interested in buying the other half of the property that is along the road next to the campground." She rested her hand on Walt's arm. "How are the negotiations for the property going?"

Walt shook his head. "This is one for the books. The seller claimed two days ago that he had someone else interested in the property. I was skeptical because he's been trying to sell me that property for ten years; I've never considered it seriously until now, so I asked our family lawyer, Nelson Decker, to do a little digging."

Stephanie set a cup and a burrito in front of Walt; after she poured his coffee, she remained at their table with the coffee pot.

"I need coffee first." Walt drained his cup.

Stephanie refilled it then raced away to refill other cups.

Walt took a gulp then ate half of his burrito. "I heard from Nelson late last night. He heard from one of our locals that the property may be jointly owned by the man's ex-wife; they were divorced three years ago. There could be a little flimflam going on here because he may not be able to sell it without her signature unless there was an agreement in the divorce settlement. Nelson plans to contact the ex-wife's lawyer who represented her in the divorce to see what he can find out, but this may be messier and drag out longer than we expected."

"That's a big surprise, Dad," Gage said.

"I've always thought that old devil was lower than a snake," Miss Jenna Lee said. "Are you going to call him on it?"

"I'd rather not tip my hand right now," Walt said. "What's the inspection schedule, Gage?"

Gage pulled out his phone. "It's good that we're finally getting together to talk. For some reason, I'd thought that our property we bought included all of the land along the road. I'm glad you're working on that. I should have thought about adding you to my calendar earlier. The general contractor will be here first thing this morning, so we can discuss our overall plan and get recommendations and estimates from him on expanding the campground. The electrician and his crew are coming later; the septic guy shows up this afternoon. I'd like to know the overall plan before we dive too deep into the details."

After Walt left, Stephanie brought the check to Gage. "Your dad asked for it, just like you said he would. I reminded him it was your turn."

On the way to the campground, Miss Jenna Lee said, "Drop me off at the office. I'll get a pot of coffee going; I have water in the small refrigerator. I've ordered a larger refrigerator, so we'll have plenty of water for the workers and a place for them to keep their lunches cool."

"That's a good idea, Aunt Jenna Lee," Gage said.

"Of course, it is." She sniffed.

While Gage helped his aunt out of his truck, Wren hopped out too.

"Thanks for the invitation to go to breakfast with you and Miss Jenna Lee, Gage. I enjoyed it."

"Thanks for going with us; I'll give you a ride to your camper," Gage said.

Wren shook her head. "I need to stretch my legs; thanks, anyway."

"Hope all the construction noise doesn't bother you while you're trying to write."

"I'll be fine; I'm totally heads-down when I write and don't hear a thing."

When Wren opened the camper door, Rascal opened his eyes then slowly rose to stretch.

"Were you sleeping this whole time? Let's go to the office. I'm hoping we'll hear why the Lonesome Trail Campground is haunted."

Before they left the camper, Wren picked up her computer and a large coffee cup to take to the office.

Rascal cleared away squirrels from their path. When they went inside, Wren shivered.

"It's a contrast coming inside after walking in that humidity, isn't it?" Miss Jenna Lee furrowed her brow. "If you're too chilly, I have a shawl you can use."

"I'll be fine." Wren pushed away her damp hair from her forehead. "I'm back to curly hair, thanks to the humidity."

"If you need a little extra help, my coffee's famous for curling your hair and your toes."

While Wren settled down with her cup of stout coffee at the small table near the large window that overlooked the campground entrance, Miss Jenna Lee confirmed reservations on her computer.

"That's my morning routine; I won't have much to do until eleven or so. I promised you the story of the haunted campground, didn't I?"

Miss Jenna Lee poured herself a cup of coffee then joined Wren at the small table. "All this happened before I was born, but my aunt told me the story her mother told her. She said I needed to know the history of the zoo and the campground. I gave you the brochure about the Lonesome Trail Railroad, so you'd know about the train. My aunt told me her mother rode the train as a child whenever she could; the passenger cars were sturdy boxes, with no roof or door. They had an opening to climb in and out and two bench seats that faced each other. Their stated capacity was four people, but my aunt said it was only true if two of them were small children because there wasn't enough room for four pairs of adult legs. The cars were painted primary colors and had the Lonesome Trail Railroad logo on the side. Did you see the engine on the sign at the diner? That was the logo."

"How long did it take the train to make a complete circuit?" Wren asked.

"Just shy of thirty minutes. It was an enjoyable ride, according to my aunt's mother."

"How close was it to the animals?" Wren asked.

"Actually, not very close at all. My three-greats-grandfather didn't want to upset the animals with the noise of the engine or the squeals of the people when they saw the animals. The animals were much closer to the campground than they were to the train. There was a walking trail for people that went through the zoo and close to the animals' outdoor recreation. The gorillas' outside area included a castle that was similar in size to my office building. The castle was on an island with a moat surrounding it. People were separated from the moat by a four-foot-tall concrete wall with peep holes for children, so they could see the castle and the gorillas; the wall had a six-foot wire fence on top of it."

"It should have been safe," Wren said.

Miss Jenna Lee nodded. "Should have been. There were several gorillas that sunned themselves in front of the castle on a regular basis, but the Grande Dame of them all was an elderly gorilla, Zuri."

"Zuri is an unusual name; very pretty."

"Zuri means beautiful in Swahili." Miss Jenna Lee smiled as she rose and poured herself more coffee. When she raised her eyebrows and the pot, Wren shook her head.

Betsy will laugh when I tell her Miss Jenna Lee drank me under the table.

"According to my aunt, a small child somehow managed to scale the wall, found a way through the wire fence, and fell into the water. The much-loved Zuri became agitated by the screams of the bystanders and broke out of her cage. The people around the moat were pointing at the water; some of them screamed for Zuri to save the baby. She climbed over the tall fence that surrounded her side of the moat and jumped into the water; the screams grew louder as she repeatedly dove under the water then resurfaced."

Wren's heart quickened as Miss Jenna Lee continued, "The elderly owner, my three-greats-grandfather, who was the engineer for the train that circled the park and zoo, rushed to see what all the commotion was about; he unlocked the fence and crossed over a small access bridge to the castle.

"When Zuri emerged from the water for the last time, the screams from the growing number of horrified zoo visitors became even more intense: she held the lifeless girl in her arms.

"Zuri lumbered to my elderly grandfather and handed the small child to him before she roared in frustration that she didn't save the little girl; Zuri beat her chest, collapsed, and died."

"What a tragic story." Tears welled up in Wren's eyes, then a stray tear slid down her cheek and dropped onto her arm. The single tear was followed by many more.

Miss Jenna Lee nodded. "It is; the child didn't survive, and Zuri died of a heart attack; after my elderly relative filled in the moat, he died while he was dismantling Zuri's cage. The family legend is that he died of a broken heart."

Miss Jenna Lee handed Wren a box of tissues after she pulled two for herself.

After Miss Jenna Lee composed herself, she said, "I haven't told the story in a long time. It's so tragic; who would want to listen?" She exhaled. "Over the years, people who have stayed at the campground have reported hearing at different times a little girl crying, even though there weren't any children camping here, the mournful roar of an animal in pain, and the wail of a lonely train whistle."

"It's not the campground that is haunted; it's the old zoo," Wren said.

"If what people have claimed to hear is true, then yes."

"This is such a sad story; why would anyone want to read it?"

Miss Jenna Lee smiled. "I like your style, Miss Weaver; you go straight to the heart just like I do. The family legend is that the ghosts of my three-greats-grandfather, Zuri, and the little girl will be happy when the railroad is rebuilt, and the moat and zoo are replaced by a park where families gather."

"Wow; no wonder Walt is determined to take back the property, but why now and not earlier?"

"Money and time, but mostly time; the family has the money, but we've never had anyone who could manage that large of a project."

Wren nodded. "Walt's retired, Gage has marketing experience, and it sounds to me like the three of you have a shared vision; this very definitely has the potential to be a successful project."

"That's what I'm thinking."

"I can write this," Wren said. "It all depends on whether Walt can buy the property that borders the campground, doesn't it?"

"Bingo."

Wren rose. "Let's go, Rascal. I need to take down copious notes then turn them into a fascinating outline."

"You'll have it done by lunchtime." Miss Jenna Lee smiled as she answered her phone.

As Wren strolled back to her camper, Rascal zoomed in large circles around the campground in case any squirrels wanted to play chicken and stay on the ground.

Wren reviewed her notes about the tiny camper. "Number one on my list is the sofa that doubles as a bed. I thought nothing could be worse than the hard bed in our first camper, but at least it was a bed. This sofa that flips open to a bed is barely big enough for me, and the only practical way to deal with it is to leave it as a bed, which means the only place I have to sit is this tight booth that surrounds the monster dinette table. There's plenty of room for a bed where the dinette is, and a small table and a chair or even two chairs would fit just fine in the space where the sofa is."

Wren groaned. "I forgot to ask Miss Jenna Lee about the wi-fi. Maybe it will be good enough for email."

Wren turned on her laptop and logged onto the campground wi-fi. She furrowed her brow. "I'm not having any problem at all with the internet. I'll ask Miss Jenna Lee if there's a connectivity problem when everybody returns to the campground."

Wren pounded the computer keys as she wrote about the bed and the inadequate refrigerator and reiterated her complaint about no oven. After she added the lack of a thermostat to control the air conditioner to her list, she stared at her screen. *I should mention that the awning is nice.*

After she sent her email, Wren jotted down brief notes in her notebook about the tragedy at the zoo then quickly typed the story that Miss Jenna Lee had told her.

Rascal opened one eye when Wren tapped her fingers on the table.

"I supposed I should write an introduction about the campground, Rascal, but right now, I can't honestly think of a reason why anyone would want to come here except for the Dry Creek Gas and Grub and the Whistle Stop."

Wren smiled. "Those are pretty good reasons, aren't they?"

She rose then listened to the construction work going on outside. She peered out the window at a large truck behind the last row and watched as a man used a piece of equipment she didn't recognize to dig a trench.

"I certainly was into the story; I didn't have any idea that anyone was around."

Wren stretched her back. "I'm stiff from being cramped at the dinette. I'd like to check out the old zoo sometime, but wouldn't that be trespassing? Let's walk up to the office and talk to Miss Jenna Lee."

When they went inside the office, Miss Jenna Lee said, "Oh good, you're here; I was just getting ready to call you." She casually slid her crossword puzzle book under the desk.

She smiled at Rascal; he trotted to her and sat, and she gave him a treat.

"Stephanie called me. The no-good skunk who is trying to sell his wife's property is at the Whistle Stop and is spouting off. I can't go myself, but I was wondering if you had a hankering for a good old-fashioned Texas taco, and if you wouldn't mind, bring one back for me too."

"I can do that."

"Of course, you can. Sit at the counter. The blow-hard is sitting at a booth near the cash register, so you'll be able to hear him just fine. If Rascal wouldn't mind, I'd enjoy his company."

Rascal flopped onto the floor near the registration desk and grinned. "Rascal would love to stay with you; I'll leave right away."

Chapter Three

Wren jogged back to her camper; she picked up her backpack and locked the camper door then sped to the Whistle Stop.

After she parked, she took in a breath then slowly exhaled. *I need to slow down a bit, so I can go inside all casual-like.*

When she sauntered inside, all the counter stools were taken.

Stephanie quietly spoke to a man, and he rose then smiled at Wren. "You here for lunch, Wren? I was saving your seat for you."

He chuckled as he strode to a table at the other end of the diner and joined a group.

"Taco for you, and one to go for Miss Jenna Lee? Whatcha drinking? Sweet tea, I bet."

"You have sweet tea? That's my favorite; I've missed it."

After Stephanie placed an oversized drink glass and a straw on the counter, she hurried to pick up an order.

"I've had that property for years." The man's voice carried over all the conversations around Wren. "It's nice and all with great potential, but I got too many irons in the fire these days to do it justice. I'm not interested in giving it away, though, in spite of what some bottom feeders might think." His chuckle sounded mean.

Stephanie stopped behind Wren and whispered, "Now you know why I told Miss Jenna Lee she couldn't come here; it had to be you."

Wren nodded. "No kidding."

"I got me a buyer that's willing to pay double what it cost me to buy, but he's not from around here. Those people from out-of-state are only interested in money. He's talking about building condos."

"Condos? Here?" a man asked. "That's nuts; where's he gonna find tenants?"

"They'd be them exclusive vacation club condos with their fancy restaurants and what they call amenities like a guard at the gate."

"Gate? They'll be fenced in like sheep?" a man asked, and the men around him chuckled.

"What a big bag of wind," one of the men at the counter muttered.

"Yeah, they'll have a tall fence to keep the riffraff out," the man said.

"Gonna keep you out, huh? That's gotta bite," another man said loudly, and the entire diner roared.

Wren's eyes widened as a heavy-set man with a red face stomped to the register and slammed money on the counter then kicked at the door just as a large man who was on his way in opened it. The men in the diner guffawed when the angry man lost his balance and stumbled out then hurried to his car. Men wiped their eyes, and the laughter died down.

"Couldn't have happened to a nicer guy," a man said, and the laughter and trash talk filled the diner.

When Stephanie brought Wren the check and a large sack with Miss Jenna Lee's taco, her face was tight with concern. "Do you think he was serious when he said there would be restaurants?"

"He was just blowing smoke, Stephanie, and doing a bad job of pretending to be a big shot."

Stephanie's smile was weak. "Thanks; I was worried."

Before Wren left, Stephanie said, "We gave you and Miss Jenna Lee a little afternoon snack; put the sack in the refrigerator after you pull out her taco."

"Thank you."

As Wren headed back to the campground, she sighed. *I am stuffed. I should have saved part of my taco for supper.*

Wren parked at her camper then hurried to the office. When she went inside, Rascal howled, and she laughed.

"I'm glad you had a good time, Rascal." Wren pulled out the taco and napkins; Miss Jenna Lee had an empty plate on her desk. While the old woman unwrapped her taco, Wren put the sack in the refrigerator.

"You talk; I'll eat," Miss Jenna Lee said.

Wren told her what the supposed owner of the property said; when she described the men's reactions, the old woman laughed. "Wish I could have been there, but I wouldn't have been able to keep my trap shut."

"Stephanie was afraid he was telling the truth; she's worried about not having a job."

"That's awful. See the damage that a man like that does without a twinge of awareness or guilt? So, who pushed him when he went out the door? You or Stephanie?" Miss Jenna Lee rubbed her hands together in glee.

"Now, I'm sorry you weren't there to prompt me; I didn't even think of it. What's his name?"

"What's in the sack you put in the refrigerator?" Miss Jenna Lee asked.

"I don't know; Stephanie said it was an afternoon snack for us, and you changed the subject on me."

"His name is Raleigh Baker." Miss Jenna Lee's eyes crinkled. "Well, is it afternoon enough for you?"

Wren hurried to the refrigerator; when she returned to the desk, Wren smacked her lips as she peered inside the sack. "Two miniature cheesecakes with two sides of cherry topping."

While they enjoyed their cheesecakes, the angry man came inside with a scowl on his face.

"I need to see Walt Navarro immediately," he roared.

Rascal growled as his hackles raised.

"I think our dog doesn't approve of the tone of your voice," Miss Jenna Lee said.

The man clenched his fists as he took a step toward Miss Jenna Lee; Rascal snarled and assumed an aggressive stance. Wren put her right hand on her waist near her holster.

"Somebody needs to do something about that dog," he muttered.

"Was that a threat against my dog?" Wren's voice was hard as she flipped her shirt out of the way of her holster and exposed the butt of her pistol.

Miss Jenna Lee set a shotgun on the desk with a thud.

"I'm filing charges," the man said.

"Good," Miss Jenna Lee said. "We caught everything you said on our security tape."

The man glanced around the room. "You can't record me without my permission."

"Where'd you suddenly get a law degree, sonny? Mail order from New York City?" Miss Jenna Lee asked.

The man slammed the door as he left; Wren exhaled at the sound of a car's tires spinning on the gravel driveway as the vehicle raced away from the office building.

"That went well, don't you think?" Miss Jenna Lee gave Rascal two treats then took a bite of her cheesecake.

"Best I've seen." Wren picked up her fork. "Have you thought about a dog to hang out with you after we leave?"

"One of the ranchers breeds dogs and has some pups. It might be nice to have someone intelligent to talk to."

"Call him. Do you have a security camera?" Wren asked.

"Heavens, no; what do I need with a security camera? I can barely remember to reset the internet server for the night schedule."

Ah ha. "Show me."

Miss Jenna Lee motioned for Wren to come around the desk.

"Here. I'm supposed to turn this dial, so it will stay on overnight."

"I don't understand why you have to..." Wren studied the dials and buttons then pointed. "This switch is on manual; what happens if we put it on automatic?"

"I don't know; what do you think?"

"I don't know either, but let's give it a try." Wren tapped the switch to automatic. "Is it okay if I adjust this dial to continuous instead of twelve hours?"

"If you think it's okay, then you go right ahead."

"I'll let you know tomorrow how it went; just remember to forget to turn the dial." Wren smiled.

"I'll write myself a note." Miss Jenna Lee tittered.

"Are you going to be okay by yourself if we leave?" Wren asked. "We'll stay until you call the rancher. What kind of dogs are they?"

"Pups."

"Okay, I'll make a list." Wren grabbed a pencil and a scrap piece of paper. "We need to know how old they are and what type of training they've had so far; the rancher should know whether..."

Miss Jenna Lee interrupted her. "I'll call; you ask the questions."

She picked up her phone. "I'm calling about those pups you've been pestering me about. Here's my interrogator."

Miss Jenna Lee beamed as she handed the phone to Wren.

"Hi, this is..."

"Hello, Wren. You talked that old brick wall into considering a dog? Good for you." The man chuckled. "They're Labrador Retriever on their mama's side, and their papa is a neighbor's standard poodle who popped over to my ranch for a social call."

"Wow. Loyal lab and smart poodle."

"Right; they're three months old, so they're still puppies, but they are housebroken and can probably be easily trained. I've got two left from the litter, and both of them are spayed females. I'll bring them by this afternoon, so y'all can decide who stays."

"Cool. Do you know what time? Rascal and I would like to be here."

"How about thirty minutes?"

"That's great."

After Wren hung up, Miss Jenna Lee narrowed her eyes. "Fill in the blanks, Wren. I take it he's coming here."

"He'll be here in thirty minutes."

"I did hear lab and poodle mix, so his pups aren't small dogs that I will fall over because I can't see them."

"I think that's a big deal," Wren said.

"I agree; you and Rascal are staying, so we can be sure they meet Rascal's approval, right?"

"Yes, so I have a question: who owns the property behind the campground and where the zoo was?"

Miss Jenna Lee glanced away. "Why do you ask?"

"I did some research. The original property was much larger than the campground and the small zoo. In fact, Mr. Baker's property doesn't include the zoo or any of the railroad tracks. His property is only the front portion of the park that was the picnic area and most of the parking lot."

Miss Jenna Lee glared at her. "Are you certain?"

"Oh, yes; I'm positive. You own the largest portion of the original property, don't you?"

"You journalist types are good researchers, aren't you? You're right about the original property being much bigger than the two that are along the road. The original zoo with the castle and moat was behind the campground, and the park with the train station was next to it."

"That's why people who were staying at the campground reported a sobbing young girl, the wild animal roar, and the distant train whistle."

"That's just conjecture..."

Wren raised her eyebrows.

Miss Jenna Lee exhaled. "Yes."

"So, how did the split in the property happen?"

"You are one nosy girl; did you know that?"

Wren giggled. "No, I didn't know that; thanks for telling me."

Miss Jenna Lee tittered. "You're welcome."

Wren raised her eyebrows at Miss Jenna Lee. "Well?"

"Not all of the family members were interested in selling the property; to keep peace in the family, the ones who wanted to sell were given what was considered to be the prime piece of real estate: the small portion of the property that fronted the road. The one family, my grandparents, that didn't want to sell retained the largest portion that had no access from the road. All the heirs were happy."

"I can't tell you how many times I've heard of relatives battling over money and completely ripping apart their once-close families; that is an absolutely amazing story," Wren said.

"Even though you can't include it in your article," Miss Jenna Lee said.

"I can't?" Wren exhaled. "Then I won't; thank you for sharing it with me. When are you going to tell Walt and Gage?"

"They'll hear about it from Nelson Decker when he reads them the will after I'm gone; for now, I want that property to remain a place of refuge for my three-greats-grandfather, the little girl, and Zuri until the campground is expanded and the family park is in operation."

Wren shrugged. "They should hear it from you. I've been wondering, is Raleigh Baker's ex-wife from the area too?"

"I almost forgot; my new accountant is on her way. My accountant, George Turner, passed away a few months ago; it was a shock because he was only a little older than Walt and Nelson: young men, as far as I'm concerned. Gage recommended Tara; evidently, he'd had some business dealings with her and told me she was an excellent accountant. I've asked her to sit in on the meetings with Walt, Gage, Nelson, and all their experts. She'll let me know the best way to manage the finances. Nelson has legal smarts and will make sure the contracts are right; Tara will make sure there's an appropriate flow for the money. I don't like getting nothing but promises for my money. She lives a little over an hour away in Waco, which is just down the road in Texas miles."

Wren giggled. "I never heard of Texas miles before, but after driving for three days to get partway across Texas, I know exactly what you're saying."

A large pickup parked in front of the office. A muscular man with a gray moustache to match his gray temples and a weathered face and hands opened the office door, and two puppies, one medium brown and the other a soft cream, darted inside in tandem and raced to Rascal. When they slid into him, he quietly woofed, and the two puppies raced back to the rancher, who chuckled as he strode to Wren with his hand out.

"I'm Ralph Carson; you must be Wren."

Wren smiled as they shook hands.

Miss Jenna Lee said, "Our puppy trainer is Rascal. He and Wren will be here a week or two."

"You'll have your work cut out for you, Rascal, if you're going to teach Coco or Luna her manners," Ralph said.

Rascal whined, and the puppies copied him.

"Why don't I take the three of them outside for a break. I have a feeling this is their first lesson," Wren said.

Wren smiled as Rascal waited while the two puppies squatted. After they'd taken care of business, Rascal ran toward the side of the office, and the puppies followed him. When they disappeared around the corner, Wren turned to watch the other side of the building. Rascal raced to Wren, and the puppies ran as fast as they could. Rascal suddenly sat in front of Wren, and the puppies copied him.

"Good job, Rascal," Wren said. "Good girls."

Wren opened the door, and Rascal led the two puppies into the office.

"Ralph is pulling a fast one on me, Wren. He claimed the two puppies will be trained faster if they learn together," Miss Jenna Lee said.

Rascal yipped, and Ralph grinned.

"You could keep one and foster the other," Ralph said.

Wren rolled her eyes.

"I suppose I could, couldn't I? They're both really cute; what do you think, Wren?" Miss Jenna Lee asked.

Wren glanced at Ralph who raised his eyebrows in surprise then narrowed his eyes as he peered at Wren.

"They'll need lots of exercise, and if they have each other to race, that takes the pressure off you. What about grooming, Mr. Ralph? Their coats aren't quite as curly as a poodle's, but they'll need extra attention and regular brushings."

"The standard poodle's rancher has an outstanding groomer. I can call her for you, Jenna Lee, but I'm sure she'll be happy to add the puppies to her weekly routine."

Miss Jenna Lee stepped out from behind her desk with both of her fists at her chest. Rascal trotted to her and sat, and Coco and Luna copied him.

"Good boy," Miss Jenna Lee gave Rascal his treat; he remained sitting, and the puppies continued to sit too.

Miss Jenna Lee broke the treat she had in her other hand in half, then gave each puppy a treat. "Good girl, Coco; good girl, Luna."

"This is absolutely amazing," Ralph whispered.

"I'll foster both of them for a month, Ralph."

"Yes, ma'am. I've got new puppy toys, new blankets, and food in my truck."

"I'll help you bring in their things," Wren said.

While Wren lifted out the small box with the puppies' toys and blankets from the backseat, Ralph said, "I was hoping she'd take a puppy because I've worried about her being alone; I sure didn't expect her to want both of them, but it's ideal for the three of them. Her claim that she'd foster both of them for a month was a knee-slapper; if I came back to pick up Coco and Luna in a month, she'd chase me off with that double-barrel shotgun she keeps under her desk."

After they went inside, Ralph said, "You might want to set up a puppy corner, Jenna Lee. Energetic puppies like these little gals go until they drop, which doesn't take very long since they're still pretty young."

After Ralph left, Miss Jenna Lee asked, "Where's the best place to set up their corner?"

"Probably behind your desk, so they can feel like they're keeping an eye on you."

While Miss Jenna Lee filled their water bowl, Wren put the large dog bed for them to share in the corner and a few of the toys on the desk. "Do you have a plastic bin or a basket for their toys? Rascal can teach them to put their toys away, so you don't have to spend all your time picking up."

"I think I have just the thing."

Wren's phone rang. *It must be time for lunch in Arizona.*

"I'll be right back to help you, Miss Jenna Lee; I have a phone call."

"Take your time; I don't move fast."

When Wren answered, Justin said, "I thought I was going to roll over to voice mail. Is now a bad time to talk?"

"Not at all. Miss Jenna Lee has two new puppies; we're going to set up a puppy corner for them, so they'll have a place to relax in the office."

"Who is Miss Jenna Lee, and tell me about the puppies."

"She's the campground owners' elderly aunt and is staffing the registration office until they can hire someone to manage the office. She's a little eccentric..."

Justin interrupted, "You think she's eccentric?"

"Very funny." Wren rolled her eyes. "You want to hear this or not?"

"Of course, I do; I like eccentric and puppies."

"The puppies are chocolate lab and standard poodle."

"Rascal's going to train them, isn't he?"

"He's already working on it."

"You probably need to get busy on your puppy corner, and I have a bunch of paperwork to review and sign. I'll talk to you later, honey."

After she went inside and set up the puppy corner, Coco and Luna explored their new spot and sniffed the basket with their toys then snuggled together on the soft dog bed and closed their eyes.

"Shall I put their food, beds, and the rest of their toys in your car for you?" Wren asked.

"Here's my keys; put everything in the trunk." Miss Jenna Lee held out her car keys.

When Wren opened the trunk, she stared. *This is almost completely filled with boxes.* Wren shifted a few boxes around then managed to add the dogs' things to the almost full trunk.

Before Wren returned to the office, a car parked in front of the building; a young woman who appeared to be ten years older than Wren stepped out of the car. She had pulled her black hair into a tight bun and wore dark aviator sunglasses and a navy suit with a white blouse and navy high heels; she carried a black leather briefcase in one hand and a tan canvas backpack in the other.

"Are you Wren? I'm Tara Chavez, Miss Jenna Lee's new accountant. Did she tell you she wanted me to join her nephew while he and the general contractor discuss the plans for renovating the campground?"

"She's been expecting you." Wren smiled as she opened the office door.

When Coco and Luna rushed to the door to greet Wren and Tara, Rascal growled, and they immediately returned to sit next to him near the desk.

Miss Jenna Lee smiled. "We're working on our manners thanks to Rascal. You've met Wren, I take it?"

"Yes, ma'am. Are the puppies visitors too?"

"Coco and Luna are my new roommates and guard dogs."

"I love their names: really easy to remember; Coco is chocolate brown, and Luna is the bright moon." Tara nodded at Rascal. "Nice to meet you, Rascal."

Rascal grinned; Coco and Luna copied him, and Tara's laugh sounded like morning chimes.

"Is Walt here? I didn't see any vehicles parked out front," Tara said.

"Not yet, but I expect him any time now."

"Good; I have a few minutes to change; I came straight here from a stuffy budget meeting with the county finance manager, as an advisor: what a fussbudget, but he knows his numbers, so it was productive overall."

When Tara came out of the women's restroom, she wore a pink and turquoise shirt, jeans, and western boots; Tara had let down her long hair then pulled her soft curls into a low ponytail. "I'm a human being now."

Tara opened her briefcase and pulled out a notepad with yellow-lined paper. After she carried her briefcase and backpack to the storage room, Tara asked, "Anything in particular you want me to focus on, Miss Jenna Lee?"

"I think Nelson will be here too, but I'd still like to make sure the interim payouts are based on measurable completion points, just like you told me. I wrote it down." Miss Jenna Lee pointed to a notepad next to her computer.

Tara nodded. "Always."

A truck then a car parked in front of the building. Miss Jenna Lee glanced out the window.

"They're here."

"I'll join them." Tara hurried toward the door, but before she opened it, she glared at Miss Jenna Lee and growled, "You didn't tell me Gage was going to be here."

"I didn't? Thought I did," Miss Jenna Lee picked up the phone.

Wren stared at her. *I didn't hear it ring.*

"Of course, you did." Tara sneered.

Miss Jenna Lee set down the phone as she sighed. "You don't have to be nice to him; just don't leave any marks."

Tara snorted. "Yes, ma'am. No marks, but I'm just tolerating him because you're such an adorable liar."

"Of course, I am."

After Tara left, Miss Jenna Lee said, "That went better than I expected."

Chapter Four

"I suppose you want to know what that's all about, Wren, but we'll save it for another time because you wanted to write, and I asked you to stay to meet the puppies with me," Miss Jenna Lee said.

Wren raised her eyebrows. *She's a master at dodging any subject she'd rather not discuss.* When Wren headed toward the door, Wren glanced at Rascal's sad look that was copied by Coco and Luna.

She giggled. "Rascal and the girls would like him to stay for a while."

"So would I," Miss Jenna Lee said.

"Okay, I'll be back later to take the three of them for a romp, but if Rascal asks to go out, I'm sure Coco and Luna will stay close to him."

After Wren turned on her laptop, she researched the drowning of the little girl and the death of Zuri and found a one-line mention of a child that drowned in a newspaper article about declining attendance to small attractions during the Cold War of the early 1950s.

I can write it as local legend. After Wren wrote the sad story of the little girl and Zuri, she stopped. *I don't want to mention the owner, so how do I work in the train whistle?*

"I need a break, so a good idea has a chance to sneak up on me." Wren giggled when she realized she was talking out loud to herself. "I'm used to Rascal being around."

Wren went outside to relax in her camping chair. After she sat for a few minutes, she sighed. *This isn't working; time to go for a walk.*

She headed toward the woods. *Maybe I can find the hidden house.*

While she made her way through the low brush, she smiled. *It is so much cooler in the shade.* As she continued walking, the trees became thicker. *It's getting darker because less sunlight is coming through the trees.*

When she turned to glance over her shoulder to be sure she still had her bearings, she stumbled and grabbed onto a tree to keep from falling. She swept away the leaves to see what she had tripped over, and her eyes widened. She pulled out her phone and shined its light onto what she'd found. *It's a rail.*

She kicked at the leaves until she found a second rail a little over two feet away. "It's train tracks."

"What did you expect? A ferryboat?" a gruff voice asked.

Wren jerked her head toward the voice and gazed at the man who was no more than three feet away from her. His arms were crossed, and he glowered at her. On his head was the signature blue and white pinstriped cap of a train engineer; his soft brown arms and face and faded blue overalls were streaked with coal dust.

"I was surprised; I heard there was a train with a three-mile-long track that went around the zoo."

"The zoo is gone; everything is gone except...what are you doing here? You have no business here."

He disappeared.

Wren rose to her feet. After she made her way through the woods back to the campground, she hurried to the office.

When she opened the door, Rascal, Coco, and Luna waited for her to come inside. After she was inside, Rascal yipped, and the two puppies bounded to Wren then flopped down; she rubbed their bellies and cooed, "Good girls."

Rascal yipped again, and the puppies rolled to their feet and sat.

Wren hugged Rascal. "You are a great trainer."

"He certainly is," Miss Jenna Lee said. "He's been working with us. Watch this."

Miss Jenna Lee strolled to the front door. "Ready for a walk?"

Coco and Luna raced to the door then stopped; Miss Jenna Lee opened the door. "Okay."

Coco and Luna bounded outside then stopped after they stepped off the porch; they quivered with anticipation as they watched Miss Jenna Lee step outside then join them. "Okay, take a lap."

The puppies raced around the building. When they returned to the front, Miss Jenna Lee motioned for them to continue, and they scrambled to get their momentum then disappeared around the corner. When they returned, Miss Jenna Lee said, "Inside."

Coco and Luna trotted inside then hurried to their water bowl.

"That was amazing," Wren said.

"It was, wasn't it?" Miss Jenna Lee beamed. "Do you care for some water?" She hurried to the storage room then returned with two bottles of water.

After she handed Wren a bottle of water, Miss Jenna Lee said, "You didn't come here just to see how awesome we are."

"I realized I had a question. Was your three-greats-grandfather's last name Navarro?"

"Why?"

"I'm not mentioning him in the article, but I was curious."

Miss Jenna Lee narrowed her eyes as she examined Wren's face. "I suppose you can't think of him as the three-greats-grandfather; yes, his last name was Navarro. One of the stipulations of his will was that the property could only be owned by one of his descendants with his last name; even if I had ever married, I would have kept Navarro as my last name, which would have been quite scandalous back in the day, by the way."

"Would he have been referred to as Mr. Navarro, or was there a title he would have used like Engineer Navarro?"

"The tourists may have called him Mr. Navarro, but everyone else would have said, 'Señor Navarro'."

"Senor Navarro?"

Miss Jenna Lee clutched her chest. "No, Wren, your Georgia accent just slaughtered Señor and the Navarro sounded like..." Miss Jenna Lee cleared her throat. "Maybe you should stick with Mister Navarro, then at least the two words will go together."

Wren nodded then drank her bottle of water. *Glad I asked.*

"I didn't realize how thirsty I was; thank you. Isn't it almost time for you to be going home?"

"I'd like to talk to Tara before she leaves, so we'll be going home closer to suppertime."

When Wren turned to leave, she noticed two boxes by the door. "Did you need those boxes to go to your car?"

"Actually, I do; those are my old crossword books from the storage cabinet. I thought I'd take them home and feed them to the shredder, which much more humane than tossing them into a dumpster. Put them on the front seat, so the puppies won't be crowded in the backseat."

After Wren returned to the office, she asked, "Ready to go, Rascal?"

Rascal turned to the puppies and licked their faces then trotted to the front door. When the puppies started to follow him, he yipped then returned to lick their faces.

Wren opened the door; as she and Rascal left, Coco and Luna whined. Rascal yipped, and each puppy yipped twice.

"Girls have to have the last word?" Wren asked.

Rascal grinned and raced ahead to their camper.

When Wren reached her camper, Tara stomped from the back section of the campground on her way to the office; her face was beet red as she glowered at Wren.

"All the Navarros are snakes," Tara fumed. "Serpientes."

"Is there anything I can do for you?" Wren asked.

"Slit their throats," Tara snapped and continued to mutter in Spanish as she stormed past Wren.

Wren stared at Tara's back. "I think minding my own business might be a good idea right now; what do you think, Rascal?"

Rascal howled.

"A mess for sure. I can't call Betsy because she'll tell me to pack up and come to Arizona. We could do that after we drop off the camper at El Paso, but I want to write this story even more now that I've met Mr. Navarro, or at least his ghost. I don't think I can slit his throat though. I am really confused. I'd ask Miss Jenna Lee what's going on, but she's the most secretive person I've ever met. Tara called her an adorable liar, and I think Tara might be right. I changed my mind: I'll call Betsy; she's sensible."

Wren exhaled; after they went inside the camper, she called Betsy.

When Betsy answered, Wren said, "I wasn't thinking straight. Are you in the middle of eating supper? Call me back."

"Whoa," Betsy said. "I just finished lunch. What's going on? You sound like a mess; Butch can take over the campground and I'll fly to...where would I fly? Texas? I think I have relatives in Amarillo; should I fly to Amarillo?"

Wren chuckled. "I got time zone twisted for a second there. I just need to vent or hear your news because I'm homesick for Arizona, so don't fly to Texas and definitely not Amarillo because I think it's maybe a two-day drive from here."

Betsy exhaled. "So, vent."

"I have the article half-written, but I'm kind of stuck until the people here do something besides take potshots at each other; I'm caught in the crossfire of a sniping war of angry words and secrets."

"Words can be dangerous; if you can't get out of the middle of it, tell me where I should fly, and I'll help you pack."

"I have to see the story come to a good resolution."

"Send me the story; maybe I can suggest something."

Wren rose from the bench seat and peered out the window; while she watched, small clouds raced to join a tall, billowing cloud. Rascal snuffled in his sleep.

"It's a super sad story," Wren said.

"I'll remember that it will end well, so I'll be okay."

"I'll send it; tell me the latest news."

"Surprisingly, there are four really different candidates for the teacher's position. I didn't think they'd find anyone; all but one have relatives in the area. One of them is from Phoenix, but he grew up in Tombstone, so he'd be a good fit for our small town. Justin scheduled a meeting for our committee at four thirty this afternoon for our first peek at their applications. He said we'd divide up our preliminary work: one person would check social media and maybe two people would check references. He's going to keep the relatives from trying to sway our decision, which is the hardest task of all, as far as I'm concerned. I'd just give them a timeout and tell them they're interfering busybodies."

Wren giggled. "I like your delicate approach; how's Socorro?"

"Give her a call; she's cranky because she's feeling better, but her doctor and Sheridan want her to take it easy for another week. So, tell me about the sniping."

"There are obviously some secrets that I have no clue what they are because the accountant for the campground was really angry at the owners of the campground: Miss Jenna Lee, her nephew, and her grandnephew. When I asked the accountant if there was anything I could do for her, she told me to slit their throats."

"Us bean counters don't mince words, do we? I'm sure she has a good reason; did she happen to mention what it was?"

"No, and I didn't think to ask."

"Is there any way you can work that into your article? It seems too dramatic to leave out."

Wren chuckled. "Can you imagine how apoplectic the illustrious editor would be? Maybe I'll find a good spot to slip it in. I'm glad I called you; I needed to talk to someone I could trust, and so far, that isn't anyone here."

"That's good; I'd be heartbroken if you loved it there, so tell them thank you from me for being so devious."

"I'm not sure I'll do that, but I will send you the article."

After they hung up, Wren opened her computer and sent her draft to Betsy with a note reminding Betsy that it will end well. Wren furrowed her brow. *At least I hope it will because otherwise I won't have an article to be published.*

Wren's phone rang. "The puppies and I are going home for the day. We'll see you tomorrow," Miss Jenna Lee said.

"Thanks for letting us know. Have a good evening."

After they hung up, Wren shook her head. *No mention of Tara or any report.*

She pulled out the box with Miranda's stories; after Wren read the first one, she smiled. *I have some ideas on what happens next.*

Wren sat at her computer and quickly copied the story into a new document with only a few changes then continued typing.

Two hours later, Rascal whined; Wren glanced at the clock. "You must be starving; I think I might be too. I really got into Miranda's story."

While Rascal ate, she closed her computer. "I need to take a break; maybe we can go for a short ride."

When the two of them went outside, Wren frowned at the dark sky. Her awning strained and flapped in the gusts of wind from the west. "I didn't even notice the wind had come up; it must have been really sudden."

She fought the wind as she took down her awning.

Humberto stopped his truck in front of her camper. "Wren, there's a tornado bearing down on us. Follow me; we have to get to a storm shelter. There's one three miles east of here."

"What about Rascal?" Wren shouted over the wind.

"He's a service dog."

Wren and Rascal jumped into her pickup. Wren followed Humberto out of the campground and stayed as close to his bumper as she dared while they sped east. When heavy rain hit them, all Wren could see was the spray from the large truck's tires. She gritted her teeth and stayed as close to the spray as she could.

When Humberto put on his left turn signal, Wren exhaled in relief. She eased off the accelerator, but still stayed close as he slowed then turned at a school. Humberto parked behind another work truck, and Wren parked behind him; she snatched up her backpack as she and Rascal scrambled out of her truck.

"This way," Humberto shouted as he grabbed Wren's arm and Rascal's collar when the wind threatened to knock down Wren.

A deputy sheriff opened a door and pulled them inside. "Glad you made it. Follow me downstairs; we're about to get slammed."

A deafening roar followed them down the narrow concrete steps until the deputy opened a door at the bottom of the stairs to a long hallway where people sat on the floor in small groups. After the deputy closed the door, Wren smiled at the normalcy of the chatter as people talked about what they were doing when the tornado siren went off and the bad storm in 2003.

"You okay?" Humberto asked as they sat next to a wall.

"We're fine; thanks for stopping for us."

"It was a fluke I was there. We had a piece of equipment break down at the jobsite; I fixed it but got grease all over my shirt and decided to change before I went to the gas station. I got a text from a buddy about the tornado."

"People here are talking about a tornado siren. I didn't hear anything like that at the campground."

"There are a few small communities around here; they would have tornado sirens. Most people have basements or home shelters."

Wren looked around. "Is this a school?"

"It's a consolidated school; my buddy told me this was the closest shelter to the campground. All the kids on this side of the county are bussed here for school."

"I'm surprised the campground doesn't have a shelter."

"Maybe it does, but the Navarros bought a campground that had been neglected for quite a few years. There's a lot of work for them to do."

"Have you heard that the campground is haunted?"

"Is that what you're writing about?"

When Wren stared at him, Humberto chuckled. "Miss Jenna Lee is proud of our resident journalist."

Wren smiled. *The only person Miss Jenna Lee is private about is herself.*

"My assignment is to visit four campgrounds that are reported to be haunted. Lonesome Trail Campground is my second one; the first was in Arizona."

"Legend has it there was a zoo and a park with a narrow-gauge railway system for a train that traveled a circuitous route where the campground is. A young zookeeper jumped into a small pond to save a child that had fallen off a bridge and into the water; she saved the child, but when she went in, she hit her head on an underwater abutment and tragically died as she climbed out of the pond. All the animals mourned for the young zookeeper, but one old gorilla was so overcome with grief that she died the next day of a broken heart, according to the legend. The owner of the zoo was the zookeeper's father and the engineer; he immediately closed the zoo to the public and cared for the animals himself until he died years later. People claim to have heard the steam whistle, a young woman laughing, and the call of the old gorilla."

"Do you know the owner's name?"

"I don't think I ever heard it. I can ask some of the locals that I work with. They'd know."

"I'd appreciate it. Is the pond still around?"

"I suspect the old man filled it in, but the bridge should still be there."

"That makes sense."

"If you're thinking about exploring the woods, you might want to get some snake boots," Humberto said. "Most of the snakes you'd come across are nonvenomous, but if you're as wary as I am about snakes, you'll wear snake boots."

"Where do I find snake boots?"

"You'd probably have to order them, but the gas station has gaiters."

Wren asked, "Gaiters?"

"Gaiters are canvas or leather coverings for protection from snakes. The ones at the gas station might be a little long for your legs but ask for help to find a pair that can be folded or cut shorter to fit you. Wear them over your boots and legs, and you'll be fine."

"I'll get a pair of gaiters."

Humberto motioned with his head toward a man who was in a quiet conversation with the deputy.

Wren watched as a man in khaki slacks and a white shirt that had probably fit him ten years and forty pounds earlier stroked his neatly trimmed beard and nodded as the deputy spoke.

The man faced the people in the hallway and announced, "Your attention, please."

A man placed his fingers in his mouth and whistled a piercing, high-pitched sound, and the room hushed.

Before he spoke, the man in the white shirt nodded at the man who whistled. "The threat of the storm is over. The school lost its roof and there is other damage; please be careful as you leave. There may be debris on the road, so stay alert. If you need a ride home, we'll help you find one. The electricity is out county-wide; we don't know when it will be restored, but extra crews are on the way."

Wren, Rascal, and Humberto were among the first to leave because they were close to the stairs. When they stepped out into the sunlight, Wren gasped at the mangled metal strewn across the parking lot; cars and trucks were on their sides or their roofs like a spoiled child had tossed them around in a temper tantrum then stomped on them. Just as startling were the few untouched cars and trucks that made the entire scene of destruction even more surreal.

Humberto smiled as he pointed to Wren's truck that didn't appear to have even a scratch. "I don't even see my work truck, but your pickup is fine. I'll gather some guys to clear a path to the road for the vehicles that are drivable. See if you can find my truck; I had some work tools that will be helpful if I need to repair any equipment. They were in a canvas work bag, but they're probably scattered."

Wren and Rascal splashed through the puddles as they searched the large parking lot. When they found Humberto's truck on its roof, Wren peered into the cab. "I don't see anything in there."

Rascal trotted to the back of the truck and barked. When Wren joined him, she knelt to get a better look then pulled out her flashlight from her backpack and shined the light into the tunnel created by the sides of the pickup and the upside-down truck bed. "I see it, Rascal, but it's too far back for me to reach."

When Rascal crawled into the void, Wren held her breath as she tried to hold the flashlight steady, so he could see the canvas bag. Rascal grabbed the handle by his teeth and slowly backed out, dragging the backpack with him. His progress was slow as he tugged because he repeatedly lost his hold on the handle. He shifted to the side of the canvas bag, grabbed with his teeth, and was able to pull more smoothly. When he cleared the truck bed, Rascal remained on his stomach as he tried to catch his breath. A woman hurried to Wren. "I found some water and a bowl for him. Not everyone realizes yet how important a man's tools will be to all of us over the next few days."

After Rascal drank his fill of water, he grinned. Wren tugged at the heavy bag then finally lifted it with two hands, but the weight was too much for her, and it slipped out of her hands. "I can't carry this; I'm not even sure I can drag it. I'll find Humberto if you'll stay with his tool bag."

When Wren found Humberto, she said, "We found your truck and the tool bag. Your truck is on its roof; Rascal dragged out the tool bag and is guarding it."

As Humberto followed Wren to his truck, he asked, "Did you say Rascal dragged it out? Is he okay? That bag is heavy."

"A woman gave us a bottle of water and a bowl for him, and he drank the bowl almost dry, so he's fine now."

When they reached Humberto's overturned truck, Rascal was lying next to the canvas bag; Rascal bounded to Wren, and she hugged him. "Good boy, Rascal."

"Thank you, Rascal." Humberto peered under his truck bed. "I couldn't have reached the tools; I would have had to wait until my truck was moved to get to them."

Humbert picked up his bag, then the three of them headed to Wren's truck. "It will be tight, but there's enough room for the cars and pickup trucks to get through; the work trucks need more room, so it will be a little while before they can get out."

As she followed the cleared path through the debris, Wren said, "I'd be nervous driving through such a narrow path with sharp metal on both sides except I'm immune after the drive to the shelter."

Humberto laughed. "I pushed it as hard as I could. I couldn't see you behind me because you were so close, but I could feel you were on my bumper."

"Really, how?"

Humberto furrowed his brow as he searched for the words to explain to Wren. "My truck got a boost from the low-pressure air bubble that developed when you were close enough to draft."

Wren giggled. "I don't understand one bit of what you said, but it sounded cool."

"It's definitely not intuitive, is it?"

Wren slowed as they approached the gas station and the diner.

Chapter Five

Humberto pointed. "The Whistle Stop lost its sign, but the building's intact."

Wren nodded. "The roof over the pumps is gone, but the gas station looks okay."

As Wren pulled into the campground, she gasped at the pile of debris that had been the office building. The first row of campers was completely demolished; the rest of the trailers in the campground were a mix of piles of metal and insulation and completely undisturbed, intact campers.

"Tornados are completely unpredictable," Humberto said quietly.

When Wren approached her site, she exhaled in relief. "My camping chairs are gone, but my camper's okay."

Humberto nodded. "Mine is too; if you need anything, come get me." Humberto pulled out a small notebook from his shirt's chest pocket. "I'll give you my cell number; call or text any time."

She added him as a contact.

After she sent him a text, she said, "Now, you have mine too. I can take you to work tomorrow, if you like."

"Thanks, Wren; I can probably catch a ride, but I'll let you know if I can't."

After Wren and Rascal went into the camper, Wren sat on the floor with Rascal and hugged him. She frowned when her stomach growled. "I just realized I didn't eat supper. I'm starving; I'll heat up the leftovers in the microwave."

Wren rose and flipped on a light switch then stared at the dark microwave. "Maybe I'll have cold leftovers; our lights work only because they run off the battery, and I'm not interested in trying to panfry the leftovers."

Rascal hurried to the door and whined.

"I'll go out with you."

While Wren examined the campground more closely, Gage sped to her site in the golf cart. "Are you okay? I came to get you as soon as I heard about the tornado, but your truck was gone. Did you find a shelter?"

"We're fine. We followed Humberto to the shelter at the school, so we were safe during the storm. Does your house have a storm cellar?"

"It does; it's not very large, but while we were sitting in the cellar, waiting for the storm to pass us, the general contractor told Dad the campground had a shelter at one time. We decided we'd look for it tomorrow and include it in our renovation and update plans. You probably noticed we don't have electricity. It's not just us; there's a county-wide outage."

"Is Miss Jenna Lee okay?"

"She's fine, and the puppies are fine; she has a storm cellar at her house." Gage cleared his throat. "I was kind of wondering if you'd do me a favor."

"Sure, what can I do?"

"I hate to ask, but would you call Tara Chavez and make sure she's okay? I'll give you her number. She and I...well, I don't think she'll hang up on you."

"Sure; I'll call her. Do you want me to tell her anything, like you're okay?"

"No, just make sure she's all right; you could ask if she needs anything."

I'm in the middle again.

"What's her number?"

Gage recited the number then hovered over her while Wren tapped in the number. While she waited for the phone to ring, she glared at Gage. "You're making me nervous."

Gage stepped back an inch; Wren rolled her eyes.

Tara answered.

"Hey, it's Wren. Are you okay?"

"I'm fine; what about you?"

"I went to the school shelter."

"I almost made it home," Tara chuckled. "I was close to the county courthouse when I heard about the tornado, so I dashed into their basement. It's good to know where the shelters are. How did you know about the school?"

"One of the guys at the campground told me; Rascal and I followed him."

"Oh, good; Rascal went with you too. Some of the shelters can't handle dogs; I guess they've had problems in the past."

"I didn't know that; Humberto told me Rascal was a service dog, so that was my mindset."

"Humberto? He's my cousin; actually, his wife is my cousin, but that makes him my cousin too. He's a really kind-hearted man. I'm not sure if he knew I was coming there today, but if you see him, tell him I'm okay."

"Will do. Are you coming back tomorrow?"

Wren glanced at Gage, whose face had paled.

"Probably, I need to talk to that old liar, Miss Jenna Lee. I'll either raise my rates or tell her to find another accountant; I haven't decided which one yet. How did you get my number?"

"Will you hang up on me if I tell you?"

"Probably."

"Then you know."

Tara chuckled. "Tell him I hung up on you; see you tomorrow."

Wren stared at her phone. "She hung up on me."

Wren heard a quiet snicker before Tara disconnected.

"I'm really sorry, but she's okay, right? Will she be here tomorrow?" Gage asked.

"She said maybe, so I don't know."

He exhaled. "Thanks for calling her; I'm relieved to know she's okay."

After Gage left, Rascal raised his eyebrows at Wren.

"Don't be such a nag; I decided if I'm going to be in the middle, then I get to choose sides. Let's go inside; I'm hungry, and I have plenty of time to eat before Justin calls."

Wren gobbled down her cold food. As she sipped on a bottle of water, she said, "I'm lucky the refrigerator switches to gas when the electricity is off. Cold leftovers aren't bad at all if you're hungry, and I can cook eggs in the morning. I'll call Betsy to see what she thought about the story."

Betsy answered before the second ring.

"I wasn't sure if I should call because Justin mentioned he'd be calling you this evening; that must be later. I read the story; I'm glad you warned me in advance that it was sad, but I still had a bit of a teary episode and had to blame allergies when a new guest showed up. I can't think of a thing that you need to change, though. It definitely sets the tone for a haunted campground."

"I'm afraid it might be a little too dark, but I can edit it later for the final. How's the teacher search going? I'll ask Justin, but I'm sure he'll just say fine."

"We had a little drama; I told you I had social media, right? That was a good call on Justin's part because one of the teachers does not have an impressive record on social media. Most of her posts were complaints about her coworkers, the parents, and the administration. I got the idea that she doesn't like anyone. I told Justin we should ask the teachers what their co-workers would say about them. The sourpuss teacher said she was highly respected and other teachers frequently came to her for advice. She's out of the running."

"That is definitely drama; you'd think people these days would have better sense, wouldn't you?"

"Her references were lukewarm, at best; no one wanted to say anything bad, but these were the references she listed, so they should have been singing her praises."

"Wow, so what's the next step for the screening committee?"

"The other three candidates have been invited to come here to meet with us and the school administration. We didn't want to overwhelm them with meeting with the entire committee, so Justin and I will meet with them. I think I got railroaded into that because Justin announced he'd like for one other person to join him, and the other two committee members simultaneously said, 'Betsy.'"

Wren chuckled. "So, when are the meetings?"

"I don't know; thank goodness the superintendent's office is taking care of that, but I think it will be fairly soon."

After they hung up, Wren jotted down some ideas she wanted to include in her new story. *I need to come up with a name for it. I need to call Socorro; maybe she'll have some ideas.*

Socorro answered. "I need you here, Wren; you have to come back. My husband and my doctor are in collusion; you could distract them for me."

Wren smiled. "Do you still have plans to expand the campground?"

"I've scaled back the expansion plans. I don't want to get any bigger than the four of us can handle with maybe some extra help with ongoing maintenance and landscaping. I'd like to add amenities like a large fenced-in dog park that is partitioned for several dogs that aren't social enough to be with a crowd. I'd also like to have a field where Rascal could chase jackrabbits without any fences in sight. Maybe that could be his private property. Sheridan mentioned updating the pool and putting in a large patio with a fire pit for people to sit around and sip beer and wine in the evening, so I talked to the owner of a food truck; he'd be interested in coming here on Fridays and Saturdays to sell tacos next to the patio. I was thinking about expanding the office to have enough space for locals to sell their crafts, but we have a lot of property; I've talked to a local woman who is interested in coordinating three or four arts and crafts events here. I thought we could build a large pavilion near the old saloon for the arts and crafts, if Thomas approves, and Betsy suggested we could make it Old West style and rent it out for weddings." Socorro chuckled. "I'm supposed to lounge around the house, so I've been making phone calls."

"It doesn't sound like to me that you've scaled back anything. I think you should assign Sheridan and your doctor some of your tasks you have in mind; they'll definitely be distracted. Never mind; that's a bad idea. You'd fire them before the day was over because they wouldn't do it right."

Socorro giggled. "You are so right, and then I'd go crazy because I wouldn't be speaking to Sheridan, so who could I boss around? Anyway, Sheridan, Betsy, Butch, and I are going to get together tomorrow to prioritize what we can do while we dream about our high falutin' plans."

After they hung up, Wren smiled. "I'm naming my new story 'High Falutin' Killers'. What do you think, Rascal?"

Rascal growled.

"I think it stinks too, but we have to start somewhere; it seems like using high falutin' at least gives us a title."

While Wren printed the new name of the story on the first page of Miranda's story as a reference, her phone rang.

"Hi, honey," Justin said. "How was your day?"

Wren frowned as thoughts raced through her mind. *I raced with a tornado and won. The accountant told me to slit everyone's throat, and I didn't, but I like her, so I'm on her side. Her cousin saved my life. I saw a ghost, and he said I don't belong here. The sweet old lady who runs the campground is a liar. I love burnt ends. I guess that doesn't count because that was yesterday.*

Wren bit her lip. "A little rough. Rascal and I spent most of the afternoon in a tornado shelter at a nearby school because of a tornado. I guess it was pretty big because there's a lot of damage. My truck and the camper are fine, though."

"That's awful. Are you sure you're okay? It wasn't a problem for Rascal to be in a tornado shelter?"

Wren smiled. "One of my campground neighbors, who showed me where the shelter was, told me Rascal was a service dog, but no one even asked."

"That's good; it's probably because you're in a small town."

"I'm sure you're right. Earlier today, I sent Betsy a very preliminary draft of my article; she agrees with me that the story is too sad, so I have a little work to do. What about you?"

"I'm very pleased with the progress of the committee. We may be able to complete our preliminary screening by early next week; after that it's up to the school board. Betsy and I think we should have a party in five and a half weeks. What do you think?"

"I'd love it."

"Besides your tornado, what's the weather like there? It's been hot here."

"It's really humid. My hair is in ringlets from the humidity."

"I can't imagine you with curls. Take a selfie and send it to me."

"Okay, but I want one of you too, and a photo of your house."

"You got it, and you send me one of Rascal."

Wren sighed. "I miss you." She frowned. *That sounded needy.*

"I miss you too; we need to be together, so we can get acquainted."

"That's it exactly. I feel like I'm peeking over a wall at what might be; I want what is and will be."

"You nailed it, honey." Justin sighed.

A tear slipped down Wren's cheek as she heard the longing in Justin's sigh.

"I'll make a list. We need to get past our first terrible misunderstanding when both of us got our feelings hurt."

"We have to do that?"

"Yes."

"Okay, I've got one for our list: we have to have our first real argument where both of us end up laughing because it was such a stupid argument."

"Good one; I'm taking notes. We have to be in a large group, and we both have the same thought at the same time and know it."

"That's good; Mom called that The Look. I can't wait until I look at you and see The Look when we smile at each other," Justin said.

"This is a great list. I need to know what vegetables you hate; what if you hate what I love?"

"Right; will you hate me forever because I truly detest beets?"

"Do you?" Wren asked.

"Yes."

"I love beets; I won't hate you forever, but I'll might roll my eyes and never understand how you couldn't love beets. I'll write it down then check it off our list."

Justin chuckled. "It's getting late there; I'll call you tomorrow."

"Thank you; beets are actually really good."

"You can't fool me; they are not at all."

After they disconnected, Wren exhaled. "I just realized I'm exhausted, Rascal, but I'm too wired to sleep. I'm supposed to take a selfie, but I'll wait until morning; the light in the camper is too harsh, and it would make me look washed out."

I wonder if I need to conserve my battery? Wren pulled out a flashlight then turned off the overhead light.

She sat on the edge of her bed with her spiral notebook and flashlight. "I have some ideas for 'High Falutin' Killers' that definitely pick up one of the threads that Miranda started."

When she woke, her flashlight had dimmed, and her notebook was on the floor. She pulled out fresh batteries from her odds and ends drawer and replaced the ones in her flashlight with fresh before she changed to her pajamas.

Chapter Six

When Wren woke the next morning, the microwave was flashing. She peered out the window. "The sun's coming up."

She flipped on the overhead light. "At least the microwave told us our electricity is back on."

Wren quickly dressed and started a pot of coffee, then she and Rascal went outside.

"The air is cool, but it sure is thick with humidity; if we want to do anything outside today, it will have to be in the morning because it's supposed to really heat up this afternoon, Rascal."

While Rascal investigated the debris around the camper, Wren watched the work trucks as they rolled out of the campground. Humberto waved from the passenger's seat of one of the trucks, and Wren smiled as she returned his wave.

After Wren and Rascal went inside, Rascal ate while Wren scrambled an egg. She ate her breakfast and stared at her list that she'd started for her and Justin.

"I don't understand why I didn't tell Justin all the details about the tornado, Rascal, except it didn't seem right over the phone."

Wren frowned at her phone when it rang. "Why is Miss Jenna Lee calling so early?"

"Is this too early for you?" Miss Jenna Lee asked. "I just checked my phone; Raleigh Baker left me a long voice mail message apologizing for his behavior yesterday. He wanted to drop by and apologize in person, and he said he had some information for me."

"When did he call?"

"I didn't think to look at the time, but I'm not sure I know how to do that without hanging up. Give me a minute. I'll call you right back if I hang up."

Wren listened while Miss Jenna Lee muttered at her phone, then they were disconnected.

Wren waited then answered her phone on the first ring.

"He called yesterday about a half hour before the storm hit. I suspect he'll be there sometime today. I'll let you know if I hear anything more. You'll be around the campground most of the day, won't you?"

"When will you be at the office?" Wren asked.

"A little later than usual. Gage told me the tornado flattened the registration building, so I needed to come in about an hour or two later than usual to give them time to set up a temporary office."

"I have a little shopping I'd like to do, but I'll be back before you get here."

After they hung up, Wren sent Justin a text. "Hope it isn't too early. Good morning!"

Her phone rang.

"Good morning yourself. I was just getting ready to text you, but talking is better. What are your plans for the day? You owe me a selfie."

"You owe me too. I'll send you one right after we hang up. Rascal and I wanted to go for a walk in the woods, but one of the other campground guests suggested I might be more comfortable if I had snake boots or gaiters, so Rascal and I are going shopping."

"I guess that would be a good idea in the thick brush."

"What about you?" Wren asked.

"The superintendent's office is having trouble coordinating all the in-person interviews. Our first one is this evening at seven; that doesn't seem ideal for the candidate because she's in Tucson and will have to drive here at the end of her day then back home alone after the interview. I'm going to talk to Betsy to see if she agrees it would make more sense if we go to Tucson because we could meet with the teacher earlier, and the teacher won't feel as rushed."

"That makes sense to me," Wren said. "I hope it works out."

"You know, you have another option instead of snake boots: you could stay out of the woods." Justin chuckled.

Wren giggled. "What a great suggestion, except it's shady and not as hot in the woods."

"I read about tall trees and shade one time; I thought it was a myth."

"It would be in southern Arizona, wouldn't it?" Wren sighed.

Justin matched her sigh. "I'll call you before we leave for Tucson. I love talking to you, honey."

"You too."

After they hung up, Wren said, "Let's stand next to the camper for our selfie, Rascal."

Wren knelt close to the steps and put her arm around Rascal. After she held up her phone, she smiled then snapped their selfie.

She chuckled as she looked at the picture then showed Rascal. "You're grinning too, Rascal."

She sent the photo by text then picked up her backpack. "Let's go to the gas station to see if I can find any snake boots or gaiters."

Before they left the campground, Wren's phone buzzed a text.

"Look, Rascal. It's Justin; I love his crooked grin, don't you?"

On the way, Wren snickered. "I never heard of gaiters before except as a shortened word for alligator. I'm glad I asked Humberto what he was talking about because I was very confused."

As she approached the gas station, she gaped at the three men on tall ladders in front of the diner. While two of them steadied the Whistle Stop sign that was only a little more scuffed up than it had been, the other man was attaching it to the building with a power tool.

"That's an absolutely awesome sight."

After she parked, Wren and Rascal hopped out of the pickup. While she went inside, Rascal sat near the door.

"You know Rascal's welcome in here anytime, Wren." The cashier stood near the door as she peered out the window at the diner. "They found the sign in a field about half a mile away; isn't that something?"

"That's absolutely amazing, and none the worse for wear either. Thanks for the offer, but I think Rascal wants to people-watch." Wren smiled as she glanced at Rascal.

Ralph came in the door and smiled as he nodded at the cashier. "You doing okay, Harper?"

"Sure am, Mr. Ralph," she said.

Ralph continued, "Wren, I didn't expect to run into you, but I saw Rascal outside when I pulled up to the pump and thought I'd pop in and say hello. Be sure to pick up some treats here for Rascal; they have some great choices. I'm on my way to Miss Jenna Lee's house to see if she needs any help. Talk to you later."

"Nice to see you," Wren said as he strode out the door.

She furrowed her brow when he walked past Rascal but didn't speak to him.

"That was odd," Wren muttered. *He probably talked to him on the way in.*

"What? You mean Mr. Ralph?" Harper asked. "He's always busy, but never too busy to come inside and say, hey. Are you looking for something special?"

"I need a pair of gaiters."

"I'll show you where they are." An elderly man with a cane and a stained Western hat appeared in an aisle. "Follow me. You going exploring back in the woods for your article?"

"Thought I would."

"Lots of kids around here hunt, so we may be able to find you a pair in the junior sizes," the man said. "Do you want canvas or leather?"

"I have no idea. What's the difference?"

"A snake is not likely to get through the leather in a strike, but leather's hot and takes longer to dry if you get it wet. A snake could strike through canvas, but the canvas is more likely to absorb the venom, and you'll still have your jeans for extra protection for your skin. Canvas isn't nearly as hot, and it is lighter than leather. There are some synthetic materials, but the gas station doesn't carry them because they're expensive. My advice is if you hear a warning rattle, go the other way."

"Probably canvas, but I guess it depends on what we find that fits me."

Wren and the man examined the shelves of junior gaiters.

"Let's just pick something for you to try on for size." The man handed Wren a pair of camouflage canvas gaiters. "These might be the right size for you."

Wren opened the pack then strapped on one over her boots and her jeans on her right leg. The man inspected the fit. "If you went a size larger, I think they might chaff your knee while you're hiking. Do you want to see what other color options are in your size?"

"No, I'll try on the other one too, but I think these are what I want."

After she had on both gaiters, she walked around the aisle. "I don't feel them rubbing, so I think this is what I want. Thanks for your help."

"Anytime, Wren. Do you have a lightweight jacket?"

"Not really; I have a sweatshirt."

"Let's find you a jacket, so you can have your arms protected from the briars."

The man strode to the far end of the aisle. "There are only a few of these light brown jackets because they're women's sizes, but they are tightly woven cotton and almost as sturdy as canvas. See if any of them fit you."

Wren tried on a jacket, but it was too large, so she selected the next smaller size. As she headed to the front of the store, the man trailed along behind her. "Keep Rascal close to you; not everyone is what they seem."

Wren frowned as she turned to ask him if he had anyone special in mind, but he had already headed back down the aisle.

After she paid for her gaiters and jacket, Wren and Rascal headed back to the campground.

"I want to explore the woods as soon as we get back because today's supposed to get hot; it will be a good excuse for me to spend the afternoon writing."

Wren and Rascal headed toward the back of the campground. She smiled at the hand-painted sign in front of the collapsed office building with the large arrow that pointed toward the laundry: "Please excuse our mess. Registration."

"Let's check out the new registration office before we go exploring, Rascal; I think it's probably in the laundry building."

Wren parked at her campground site, then she and Rascal hurried to the nearby laundry building.

When she went inside, only two washers and dryers were left in the far corner of the laundry room. An electrician was rewiring to accommodate the new registration desk while Gage stained the desk, and Walt hung blinds on the windows. The walls had been freshly painted pale yellow, and the trim around the windows was painted the same blue as a field of bluebells. The concrete floor had been overlaid with dark, wide planks of engineered wood laminate.

"Hey, Wren. Aunt Jenna Lee will be here in about an hour, so we're racing against the clock." Gage grinned as he stretched his back.

"This is really nice," Wren said. "Miss Jenna Lee will love it."

"One of our friends is bringing some potted plants to liven up the place, and another friend is picking up a round table, two chairs, and a small armoire to set up a coffee station from another friend," Gage said.

"Gage woke practically the entire county before daybreak this morning to help us get the new registration office ready for Aunt Jenna Lee," Walt said.

"I've ordered a new wi-fi system for the campground," Gage said, "but in the meantime, I changed the password on my system at the house to the same as the campground's. The signal isn't strong enough to reach all the sites, but I think you'll pick it up okay at your campsite because we're using it here in the office. I had a nightly backup of the reservation system and an extra computer, so we were able to get that set up first thing."

"That's really impressive."

"Thanks, Wren." Gage resumed staining the desk. After Wren and Rascal returned to their camper, she put on her new gaiters and jacket and stuck her leather gloves in her jacket pocket.

While Wren and Rascal walked to the woods behind the campground, she listened to the sparrows and the thrushes as they trilled through their morning songs. "No rain at least for a while, according to the birds," she said.

Wren and Rascal made their way through the trees and brush almost directly behind the campground. "We're looking for a moat or a bridge, Rascal."

When they came to a wooden bridge that was supported by cement pillars surrounded by large river rocks and spanned a pond with clear water, Wren said, "This is a beautiful bridge. I wonder if the pond is fed by an underground river."

"Not many people think about that."

Wren recognized the engineer's voice. "This is really nice."

A mournful roar echoed in the woods.

"Did I say something that upset her?" Wren glanced around but didn't see the engineer.

"It isn't you; you'll see. You shouldn't be here." He stood in the middle of the bridge with his arms crossed.

"Is the bridge safe to walk on?"

"It is for you but not today."

Wren shuddered at the sorrow in the next even louder mournful roar. "I'll leave for now."

"Be careful; not everyone has your best interests at heart," the engineer growled.

Wren frowned as she turned back. *That's very similar to what the old man in the gas station said.*

As she and Rascal headed back, Rascal took the lead.

"That's not the way, is it?" Wren asked. "Aren't you going away from the campground and toward the other property?"

Rascal glanced back at her then continued in the same direction. Wren glanced back then continued to follow him. When Rascal disappeared in the brush, Wren stopped and called him; he didn't answer, so she pushed through the brush in the direction where she last saw him.

Her chest tightened. *He's never done this before; where could he have gone? Am I lost, or is he lost?*

Rascal barked.

"I hear you," Wren called out and headed toward the sound. The brush wasn't as thick in the direction she was heading, so she hurried as he barked again.

When she joined him, Rascal barked and headed in a new direction.

Wren rubbed her forehead then hurried to catch up with him. *I think we're going toward the frontage road, but I might be turned around.*

She briefly lost sight of him as he dashed ahead, but when he barked repeatedly and almost frantically, she ran to him.

She abruptly stopped and stared at the body under a small fallen tree. "It's Raleigh Baker; he must have gotten caught back here in the storm."

"You're wrong. He was stabbed in the back and dragged here," the engineer said. "See the fresh marks on that tree? It was cut down."

Wren stared at the tree. "You're right; I see it now. Take me to the road, Rascal. I need to call nine-one-one."

Wren gritted her teeth and examined the body from where she stood. *His clothes are dry; he was murdered after the storm.*

"Let's go, Rascal."

Rascal maintained a fast pace through the trees but slow enough that Wren could keep up with him. Her eyes widened when they stepped into the clearing.

"We're at the campground; I expected we'd be on the other property somewhere. Let's go to the camper, Rascal; I'll call from there."

After they were inside the camper, Wren called nine-one-one. "This is Wren..."

"Hi, Wren; are you okay?" the dispatcher asked.

"I'm fine; Rascal and I went for a walk in the woods behind the campground, and we found a man who is deceased."

"You found a dead man in the woods? I'll send a deputy there immediately. You're certain he's dead? Shall I send an ambulance too?"

"I'm certain he's dead, but you could send an ambulance if that's protocol or something."

"The deputy is on the way, and the sheriff will be right behind him. I'll let them decide if they want an ambulance. I know you've only been here a few days, so I'm sure you have no idea who it is; do you?"

Wren frowned. *Should I go with the flow?*

"It's Raleigh Baker. I was in the diner yesterday morning when he caused kind of a scene; when I told Miss Jenna Lee about it, she told me his name."

"I heard about that. It sounded like he was downright ugly. Could you tell whether it was a tragic accident?"

"I really don't know; I didn't get too close."

"I don't blame you a bit for that, honey. Are you sure you're okay?"

"I'm doing all right."

Wren glanced at her bed. *I need to fold my bedsheets and flip that back to a sofa before anyone arrives.*

"The deputy will be there in about five minutes."

"Is it okay if I get a glass of water?"

"Heavens, yes. I'll let you go, so you can compose yourself. Now you call back if you need anything, you hear?"

"Yes, ma'am."

After they hung up, Wren quickly folded her sheets and put them into the overhead cabinet then folded up the sections, flipped up the legs, and added the back cushions, so that her bed was transformed to its daytime duty as a small sofa.

She poured herself a cup of coffee then took a sip. *Only tepid, not too bad.* She opened her laptop and sat at the dining table with her coffee and checked her email.

She read the new email from Charlie. "Thanks for the RV review. The CEO thinks we're doing an awesome job." Wren rolled her eyes. *We, Charlie?*

Charlie continued, "Just thought I'd check in to see if you had an idea when you'd be sending a draft for review. The editor is..."

Wren slammed her laptop lid with a loud snap. "The editor is a jerk, and I'll have to get the word of the day for you from Miss Jenna Lee, Charlie."

"Time for 'High Falutin' Killers'." Wren opened her laptop and picked up the story where she'd left off.

When she heard a vehicle park in front of her camper, she quickly found a stopping place in the story, saved it, then closed her laptop. She opened the camper door as the long-legged deputy climbed out of his county sheriff's deputy pickup.

Rascal dashed past her and nosed the deputy's hand in greeting; Wren stood in the doorway. "Would you like to come in, Deputy?"

After he scratched Rascal's ear and was inside, the deputy's head almost bumped the ceiling. "Would you care for some coffee? I can microwave a cup for you."

"I'm fine. Can you tell me how you happened to find the deceased?"

"Rascal and I went for a walk in the woods. Rascal actually found him and barked for me. When I found Rascal, I saw the dead man."

"Did you notice anything special?"

"Not really. I recognized him. It's Raleigh Baker. A tree was across his body, but his clothes were dry, so he obviously died after the storm."

The deputy peered at her. "Can you show me where he is?"

"I probably can't without Rascal; I got turned around in the woods."

"There are no real paths or anything, are there?"

Not anymore. Wren shook her head.

When they stepped out of the camper, the sheriff pulled in and parked next to the deputy's pickup.

"Nice to meet you, Miss Weaver, except for the circumstances." The sheriff stepped out of his cruiser.

"You too, Sheriff. Call me Wren."

"I can do that, Wren. So, where's our deceased?"

"In the woods; I can't really show you because I got disoriented, but Rascal can take us right to him."

"Well then, Rascal, let's go."

Rascal trotted to the edge of the woods and waited for the three of them then darted into the woods when they were close. Wren led the way behind Rascal. The deputy stayed with her, and the sheriff waved them on while he pulled out his phone.

After Rascal, Wren, and the deputy reached Baker, the deputy nodded. "Dead, for sure. The sheriff will release you, Wren, so you can go back to your camper. I'll write up your statement from my notes then bring you a copy to review."

"Thanks; I have quite a bit of writing to do today."

When the sheriff joined them, he said, "A Texas Ranger will be here in about thirty to forty minutes. Do you suppose Rascal will show him where we are?"

"Rascal and I could do that."

"I'll let him know."

"I have Miss Weaver's statement, Sheriff," the deputy said.

"Good. Wren, you and Rascal can go back to your camper; I'd appreciate it if you'd show the ranger where we are."

As Wren and Rascal headed toward the camper, the sheriff said, "Let me read your notes."

When they reached the camper, Wren said, "I'm glad we didn't have to stay in the woods and wait, Rascal. It was too buggy."

While she waited for the Texas Ranger, Wren quickly typed the story that Humberto had told her then sent it to Betsy with a note that it was a different version of the zoo legend.

"I think I'll work on the ideal conclusion for my current article. Maybe I can use parts of it later."

Wren had typed half a page when she was interrupted by a knock at her door; Rascal whined.

"Thanks, Rascal. It's good to know it's not a bad guy at our door." Wren opened the door.

The middle-aged Texas Ranger smiled. "Nope; not a bad guy. Are you Wren Weaver?"

Wren felt her face warm as she nodded. "Rascal and I will show you where the sheriff and deputy are."

Wren put on the lightweight jacket before she left the camper. Rascal trotted ahead of Wren and the ranger but stayed within sight, so they could follow him.

When they reached the sheriff and the deputy, Wren hung back. The deputy nodded at her and smiled. She returned his smile with a weak one.

"Deputy, give your report while I walk Miss Weaver back to her camper," the sheriff said.

The deputy's smile immediately flipped to a frown. "Yes, sir."

On the way back, the sheriff said, "You have an admirer, Wren. My deputy keeps talking about how rare it is for a pretty girl to be smart."

"That's really nice of him," she said.

The sheriff nodded. "You're already spoken for, aren't you? Is the lucky guy in Arizona or Georgia?"

Wren stared at the sheriff.

"Didn't mean to pry; forget I said anything."

"Is it that obvious?"

"Is to me; we've got young ladies all over the county who have set their caps at my deputy, and he's never mentioned any of them; you've been polite to him, but I haven't spotted a hint of interest on your part."

"I'm not sure I'm spoken for, but I have unfinished business in Arizona."

"Good for you," the sheriff said. "Now, this is my prejudice coming out and my nosy side asking, is he a peace officer?"

The sheriff held up his hand. "Never mind, don't answer because it's absolutely none of my business."

Wren grinned.

The sheriff smiled. "I'm sure things will work out just fine."

When they reached Wren's camper, the sheriff said, "I'll talk to Miss Jenna Lee, then I'll talk to Walt and Gage before I leave."

He handed Wren a business card. "I have your cell number because you called the dispatcher. My cell phone number is on the back. Call or text any time at all; I'll know it's you."

Wren stuck his card in her back pocket. "Thanks."

After he left, Wren said, "Let's go inside, Rascal; I know exactly what happens next in 'High Falutin' Killers', but I need to write it down right away because I might forget."

Wren's fingers flew across the keyboard in a heroic attempt to keep up with the story as it unfolded in Wren's head.

When Rascal whined, Wren blinked.

"I was really deep into the story; what time is it?" Wren glanced at her phone. "Wow, I've been sitting in front of my laptop with only my fingers moving for two hours; let's go see Miss Jenna Lee."

When Wren opened the door at the new registration building, Coco and Luna yipped and scrambled to greet Rascal. Wren held the door open for them, and the puppies trotted along behind Rascal as he went outside.

"Welcome to my new digs, Wren. What do you think?" Miss Jenna Lee asked.

Wren smiled as she surveyed the new registration office. "This is absolutely perfect." Her eyes widened at the bouquet of roses on the desk. "Your roses are beautiful; they're just the right touch for a grand opening."

"They are nice, aren't they? They were delivered just as I arrived."

"There's a card," Wren said.

"Oh, I didn't notice it; I'm sure they're from Walt and Gage. The sheriff stopped by and told me you found Raleigh Baker in the woods behind the campground. I've never been a Raleigh Baker fan, but it was still a shock. Are you okay?"

"I'm okay. Rascal and I went for a walk, and Rascal found him."

"I was waiting for you to come see my new office; Walt and Gage must have worked all night to get this up and ready for business this morning. Don't you love my coffee nook? How about a cup?"

"I'd love it."

Miss Jenna Lee poured two cups of coffee; Wren took her cup to the small table and sat down.

Miss Jenna Lee returned to her seat behind the desk. "I called Tara this morning and got an earful. Evidently, she and Gage dated for a while then didn't anymore because Gage is a snake. That's all she would say, but my money's on a misunderstanding."

"That might explain why she left in such a huff yesterday, so where does that leave you as far as the campground upgrade is concerned?" Wren asked.

"Not in the best of positions. Tara threatened to quit but finally agreed to be my accountant as long as she deals only with me. That definitely created a huge hole in my plan for her to participate in the project, but she did agree to review any documents from the general contractor."

"Do you expect Tara to come see you today?"

"I'd like for her to, but I didn't want to push my luck, so I didn't ask, and she didn't say."

"While I was at the school shelter yesterday during the tornado, I heard a different version of the incident at the zoo."

Chapter Seven

"You did, did you?" Miss Jenna Lee glanced out the window close to her desk. "Do you suppose the puppies are okay? Should I call them inside?"

She rose and opened the door. "I see them. The three of them are relaxing in the shade."

Wren continued, "The version I heard said it was the engineer's daughter who died, not a toddler who had come to visit the zoo."

"Stories about what happened a long time ago sometimes get changed in the retelling from one generation to the next."

"So, why did you change the story?"

Miss Jenna Lee growled, "That's quite presumptuous…"

Wren raised her eyebrows.

The old woman sighed. "The zookeeper was Señor Navarro's youngest daughter. His oldest daughter blamed her father for her sister's death; the next oldest daughter sided with her sister, while the next youngest child, a boy, sided with their father. It was a horrible accident, and it ripped the family apart. The family is still split to the point that I have cousins that probably live near here, but I don't even know their names."

Wren shook her head slowly. "That's such a shame. I agree with you that stories are passed down with changes along the way. If I use the story, it will be your version. What about Zuri?"

"She did die of a broken heart, and truthfully, so did Señor Navarro. He fell ill immediately after the accident and never recovered."

"The two versions are quite similar except for the relationship between the zookeeper and the engineer, and that doesn't add to the story. I do have a question: Mr. Navarro's will specified only someone with the surname Navarro could inherit; weren't the sisters also angry about that?"

"Not at all; it had been like that for generations."

Wren sipped her strong coffee. *Maybe the article will catch the eye of some of the relatives.* She sighed. *That's a dream.*

"Wren, do you suppose you could bring in my boxes from my car? I found some boxes in my storage closet at home, so I thought I could go through them here when I'm not busy. They're in the trunk; here are my keys."

Wren narrowed her eyes when she opened the trunk. *These are the boxes she took home before the tornado.*

While Wren brought in the boxes and put them in a neat stack behind the registration desk, she said, "These are the boxes that you took home before the tornado."

Miss Jenna Lee narrowed her eyes; her voice was stern. "I had an ache in my little toe, so I was certain a storm was coming; no one ever believes me."

Wren nodded then took a quick peek inside a box before she stood up. *There's more to it than that. These are crossword puzzle booklets.*

Wren straightened her back then headed toward the front door as Miss Jenna Lee hurried to take her place behind her desk.

Gage came into the registration office with Rascal, Coco, and Luna on his heels. "Do you have any treats, Aunt Jenna Lee? I might need to borrow three."

Miss Jenna Lee glared at him. "Shouldn't you have checked first before you promised them? Of course, I do."

Miss Jenna Lee set her treat bowl on the desk, and Gage helped himself to three.

Gage raised his eyebrows at the puppies as they jumped on him to get his attention. "Rascal first."

When Rascal sat, the puppies did too.

Gage gave treats to Rascal, Coco, and Luna. Rascal yipped his thanks, and the puppies copied him.

"You're a remarkable trainer, Rascal," Gage said.

Rascal stretched out on the cool floor, and the puppies flopped down on either side of him.

Gage put a thick folder on the registration desk. "Aunt Jenna Lee, Dad said you needed to see these documents from the general contractor; it's the contractor's recommendation for projects and the order and schedule for each project. Our lawyer already reviewed them; we're all getting together to go over them. The general contractor will be here tomorrow for any final revisions; he and Dad are anxious for the projects to begin."

"I want Tara to review them."

"I ordered you a new printer that also scans, but it won't be here until the middle of next week," Gage said.

"I'll call her; maybe she can come here and have lunch with me."

"Let me know, and I'll pick up lunch," Gage said.

When Miss Jenna Lee scowled, Gage sighed. "She already told me she'd leave if she sees me; I have to stay out of sight. Wren, would it be okay if I drop off lunch with you, so you could bring it here?"

Back in the middle again, but it sounds like I'm included in lunch and can talk to Tara.

"Sure."

After Gage left, Wren asked, "Do you know what the problem is between Gage and Tara?"

Miss Jenna Lee's eyes sparkled. "Yes. I'm on a new kick: I'm trying out that telling the truth thing."

That will be different. "Will you tell me?"

Miss Jenna Lee cackled. "No."

"You don't really know, do you?" Wren growled.

"No, but that was fun." Miss Jenna Lee picked up her phone then stared at it. "Why don't you call her?"

"Nope; I am not getting into the middle of this." Wren put her nose in the air and sniffed.

Miss Jenna Lee drummed a rhythmic beat on the top of the desk with her fingers. "Why not?"

"Still not the middle."

Miss Jenna Lee picked up her phone and held it close to her face as she peered at the phone and tapped a number.

"Tara, Wren told me to call you. Would you like to have lunch with us? I'll have the papers from the general contractor for your review."

Miss Jenna Lee held out the phone to Wren.

"Here, she wants to talk to you."

Wren exhaled. "Hello, Tara."

"So, tell that adorable liar I have another meeting. What time should I be there?"

"I can think of dozens of reasons you'd want to read the contract."

"Okay, got it; I'll be there at noon. See you."

"She hung up on me again," Wren said.

"Well?"

"She had another meeting; just in case she decides to reschedule or cancel it, Gage could deliver lunch to my camper by noon."

Miss Jenna Lee rubbed her hands together. "That's what we'll do. If she doesn't show up, then I'll have a nice sandwich for supper."

"Do you have Tara's email? I could scan in the documents for you and send them to Tara; maybe she'd have time to review them before she comes here."

"I didn't know you could do that; maybe that might be a good enough nudge for her to come here."

Wren left her empty cup on the table and strolled to the registration desk. "I saw Mr. Ralph this morning at the gas station; he said he was on his way to help you. Is your house okay?"

"Really? The house is fine; he's an old worry wart. He checks on me all the time; he's actually right handy to have around when I lock myself out of my safe; I gave his wife a key ages ago. Smartest thing I ever did."

Wren pulled the card from the bouquet then turned to Miss Jenna Lee. "Do you want to open your card?"

"Sure; more coffee?"

"I'll pour." Wren handed the card to Miss Jenna Lee.

As she picked up the pot to refill their cups, Miss Jenna Lee gasped.

When Wren turned to see what was wrong, the old woman's face was pale as she clutched the registration desk.

Wren quickly set down the pot then hurried to Miss Jenna Lee and helped her sit on her stool. "Should I call for an ambulance?"

Miss Jenna Lee exhaled. "No, it was just a shock." She handed the card to Wren.

Wren's eyebrows raised as she read the card. "My behavior was inexcusable; please forgive me. Raleigh Baker."

"This seems totally out of character," Wren said.

"He could be a smooth talker when he wanted to," Miss Jenna Lee said. "He was like a cobra: all charming words and engaging smiles until he decided to strike. He had a reason to talk to me, but we'll never know now what he had up his sleeve."

"Are you going to call the sheriff?"

"It seems kind of weak to call because Baker sent me flowers."

"We don't know; doesn't seem like it would hurt," Wren said.

"I'll think about it." Miss Jenna Lee stared out the window.

Sure you will. Wren refilled Miss Jenna Lee's cup and washed hers then headed to the door. "Rascal and I will be back with lunch."

"Wait." Miss Jenna Lee carefully printed Tara's email address in large, block letters with a permanent marker on the folder of documents from the general contractor then held it out to Wren.

Wren took the folder; when Rascal followed Wren to the door, Cora and Luna whined.

"Can he stay?" Miss Jenna Lee asked. She and the puppies gazed at Wren with the same look of hope.

Wren rolled her eyes at the three pitiful faces. "It's up to Rascal."

Rascal grinned then yipped, and the puppies rushed to join him.

When Wren opened the door, the three of them trooped out; she chuckled. "I guess they're going to get some outside time."

After Wren scanned the documents and emailed them to Tara, she sent Tara a text. "Emailed you the docs from the general contractor."

Tara replied, "Perfect. Thanks."

Before Wren closed her email, a new email arrived from Charlie. *I'm not certain I'm in the mood to hear from Charlie.* She chuckled. "Which means I should definitely open the email."

Charlie wrote, "Congratulations to us, Wren. The printer had a cancelation, so the print version of the magazine will be shipped on Monday; I was waiting to time our electronic version in conjunction with the print version, so it is scheduled to be sent to our subscribers tomorrow. Our editor has another commitment later next week, so if you could send me your final article by tomorrow afternoon, he'll be able to review before he leaves because he won't be available for two weeks."

Wren stared at the email. "I certainly can't answer this today. I'll read it again in the morning to see if there is anything nice I can say."

Wren stepped outside the camper and stared at the clear sky as she listened to the cicadas. *Wait a minute; I don't have to say anything nice; I just don't care to be mean. I'll think about it.*

Wren went back inside and reviewed the contractor's documents and schedule; after she rewrote her travel article from start to finish by adding the expected plans and schedule for the campground improvements, she set it aside to review later. *I still need to rewrite the first part and polish the ending.*

Wren's phone rang.

When she answered, Tara said, "I just heard about Raleigh's death; the investigator is coming to my office to talk to me later this morning, so I'm not so certain that I'll be coming to the campground after all. That man was nothing but trouble the entire time we were married; I thought I was shed of him, but he's still causing problems for me. I'll talk to you later." Tara disconnected.

Wren's mouth was still open as she stared at the phone. She snapped her jaw shut and shook her head. "Why didn't Miss Jenna Lee tell me that Tara was Raleigh Baker's ex-wife? Why would that be a big secret? Walt said the property he wanted to buy was in the ex-wife's name too, so why didn't he mention Tara? This place is so complicated for the small number of people that are around here. Seems like everyone is hiding something, or am I becoming too suspicious? I'll work on 'High Falutin' Killers' to relax."

She opened the story and read the last page she had written. "We need a little twist now."

Her fingers flew over the keys, and she chuckled as the story followed an unexpected path. After an hour, she rose from the bench seat and stretched.

"The man at the gas station who helped me with the gaiters said not everyone is what they seem; that's for sure around here."

She furrowed her brow then shuddered. "Something's bothering me, but I don't know what it is. He also told me to keep Rascal close." Wren hurried to the new registration office.

When she went inside, Rascal and the puppies greeted her.

Miss Jenna Lee smiled. "I suspect Rascal is especially happy to see you. It wears me out just watching Coco and Luna, and he's been playing with them nonstop."

Wren smiled; as she scratched Rascal's ear and rubbed the puppies' bellies, she asked, "Ready to go back to the camper and be off duty, Rascal?"

Rascal yipped, and the puppies whined.

"You two need a nap," Wren said. The puppies raced to their dog bed.

As Wren and Rascal strolled back to the camper, a large truck rolled toward the far end of the campground.

"Looks like they'll be ready to start on the updates as soon as the contract is signed."

When two more trucks turned at the campground and followed the first one, Wren said, "I guess Miss Jenna Lee signed the contract after all. I'd say it's odd that she didn't mention it, but she never mentions anything that has to do with herself. I wonder if that means she got the okay from Tara."

Wren's phone rang before she and Rascal reached the camper. She sat on the camper step as she answered Betsy's call, and Rascal flopped down next to her and closed his eyes.

"Justin just called me; we're going to Tucson to interview one of the teachers. It makes total sense to me, but we agreed that if there is a second round, our applicants will have to come to Hidden Gulch. If they're considering commuting, we want them to know what the drive will be like. I didn't participate with any of the phone interviews, but I still have a pretty strong impression of their different personalities from social media. It will be interesting to see if they match their internet self in person."

"I never thought about that before; I can't wait to hear what you discover."

"I read the second account of the zoo at the campground. The first story was more of a story; the second version sounded more realistic to me, but I can't explain why," Betsy said.

"That's really perceptive. The first story is more fictionalized, and the second is probably more factual."

"Oh, dear, so which way are you going?"

"There could be some fallout with the second version; I had to remind myself the article is for entertainment not a news exposé. I think I can write something that's a mix that is still faithful to the original event."

"Do you know the original story?"

Wren chuckled. "Maybe; I heard a third version."

"I guess that's only to be expected when it comes to a legend."

"I think I may be trying too hard to make this too much like the article for the Forgotten Oasis Campground. This haunted campground is dripping with secrets, intrigue, and unresolved conflicts; maybe that's their draw. I'll have to think about it." Wren snickered. "The article won't be dry, that's for sure."

"I can't wait to read it; what are you going to call it? 'Lonesome Trails Never End'?"

"That's good, Betsy; even if it's not the title, it could be the theme. I have all the facts to write the article; the only thing I'm missing is why should people flock to the Lonesome Trails Campground?"

"Don't forget it's more than the campground; didn't you say it's going to have a park? Will it have picnic areas? A playground area for kids? A large dog park? Those amenities will expand the customer base beyond campers."

"Perfect; I have the overall schedule for the update of the campground, but that doesn't include anything new, as far as I could tell; I'll talk to the owners about future plans."

After they hung up, Wren jotted down notes.

"I wonder if Gage is still going to bring lunch here; that would be a perfect time to ask him what the future plans are and maybe to even put in a pitch for a dog park, right, Rascal?"

Wren opened 'High Falutin' Killers' and picked up where she'd left off. After an hour, she stared at the last paragraph she'd written. "I know what happens next, but I'm stuck; how do I get there from here?"

Rascal barked.

"I can work with that: a dog barks; or should the dog howl?"

Rascal closed his eyes.

While Wren tried to decide, her phone rang.

"Hey, it's me," Tara said. "Turns out I'm not the best suspect after all, so no jail for me. I'll be there for lunch. I want you there when I talk to Miss Jenna Lee because I found something that doesn't make sense, and you know how she is."

"No kidding; look up diversion in the dictionary, and Miss Jenna Lee's picture would take up the entire page."

Tara chuckled. "Exactly; I like how you toss around those words like a drunken cook slinging hash."

Wren laughed. "Now, you're scaring me; you're taking over my job, aren't you?"

"Never in a million years. I'll see you at lunch."

After they hung up, Wren said, "I need to build up the camaraderie in the first part of my article, so it's a little less impersonal; right now it reads that a girl, an old gorilla, and an old man died. The End. When I glossed over the strong connection among the three of them, I didn't give the reader the chance to feel the emotional bond that was the core of the story."

Wren jumped onto her computer and began to type furiously as she revealed the friendships and caring among the three who died.

She was startled by a tap at her door. Rascal raised his head and watched her as she saved her document then rushed to the door. "Must not be a killer."

She opened the door, and her eyes widened at the ranger who chuckled.

She laughed. "So far, you seemed to be passing some kind of hearing test. Would you like to come in?"

As he came inside, she asked, "Is your hearing that good, or is this camper that flimsy?"

"I've always been accused of having remarkable hearing, and your window in the door has slid open about a half inch."

"Why didn't you tell me last time?"

His eyes twinkled. "You didn't ask."

Wren rolled her eyes. "Would you like to sit?"

"No, I just stopped by for a quick question. What was your first impression when you found the dead man?"

"That he'd been caught in the storm, and the tree fell and killed him."

"What changed your mind?"

"His clothes were dry."

"Couldn't the tree have fallen on him after the storm?"

"No, the tree didn't break; it was chopped down with an ax."

"How long were you next to the body?"

"Maybe two or three minutes."

"All that in two or three minutes?"

"Just like any other normal person. Why?"

"The deputy told me that's what you saw in such a short time. He was amazed because he didn't see the scene the way you did, and neither did the sheriff, until they reread the deputy's notes. You asked me about my hearing; I'm asking you about your observation skills. How did you learn to process so quickly?"

Wren cocked her head. "I guess the only way I can explain it is that I look at something and ask why; the second question I ask myself is why am I wrong?"

The ranger nodded. "Your why takes you to the obvious answer; your why am I wrong pulls it apart. This wasn't an idle question, Wren. I'm an instructor and would love to challenge our students to think like you do. Not many will get it, but some will; for the record, I do."

The ranger smiled as he left.

"My grandma would say, 'Don't that beat all.' Of course, now I'll confuse myself and ask why am I wrong first or something." Wren checked the window in her door and slid it closed then latched it.

She sat down in front of her computer and picked up where she'd left off.

When the next tap interrupted her, Rascal rose and stood at the door. "A friend," she whispered.

Rascal yipped, and she opened the door.

Gage grinned. "Ready for lunch, milady?"

"Sure, as long as there are no towers or dragons involved."

Gage chuckled. "Aunt Jenna Lee is the dragon in our family, and you've soothed her spirits."

As they strolled toward the laundry building, Wren asked, "What happened between you and Tara?"

Chapter Eight

Gage exhaled. "Not anything I'm very proud of. We were getting to be...really close, and I panicked. I've always been a love 'em and leave 'em kind of guy, but suddenly, that wasn't what I wanted, and it scared me. I handled it in the worst possible way: I made a huge mistake then kind of disappeared."

"Ouch."

"Right; there's just no good way to tell her how sorry..." Gage handed Wren the large sack with their sandwiches. "Thanks for listening. I'd do anything if I could make it up to her, but I blew it, and I'm getting exactly what I deserve."

Wren nodded. "When I asked her what I could do for her, she said I could slit your throat."

Gage laughed as he walked away. "That's Tara; maybe there's hope for me yet."

That made as much sense as some of the things that Miss Jenna Lee says; must be genetic.

When Wren opened the door to the registration office, Coco and Luna were waiting at the door. Rascal yipped then led them on a chase around the building; Wren put the large sack on the small table.

"I knew you two were on your way because Coco and Luna were sleeping then suddenly jumped up and stood next to the desk while they watched the door." Miss Jenna Lee beamed. "My two girls are just as smart as they can be. They alerted when Nelson Decker came to the door earlier then growled real quiet-like when he came inside. They quieted down when I told them it was okay, but those two little cuties stood guard between me and him. Do you care for some coffee?"

"No, thank you." Wren smiled and suppressed a shudder at the thought of how bitter the strong coffee that had been sitting on the warmer all morning would be.

"I found an old water pitcher that my mother used to use and brought it here, so I can keep the girls' water bowl filled. I was having trouble with spilling it when I filled it at the sink then carried it in here and put it on the floor." Miss Jenna Lee pointed to a small cabinet near the dogs' large bed. "I store a little dog food and their snacks in there too. What do you think?"

Wren strode to the cabinet and admired the white ceramic pitcher. "I love the tiny painted flowers; it's perfect for Coco and Luna."

"I thought so too. Nelson Decker said I had to sign the papers right away, so the work could begin, but I told him I intended to discuss the proposal with Tara before I signed anything. When he stepped toward me in a way that I thought was a little aggressive, Coco bared her teeth, and Luna's hackles raised, so he backed away. I didn't mind because I have always felt like he was bad about invading my personal space; I told them they were good girls, and Nelson's face got red, but he left. Was that the wrong thing to do?"

"Not at all; sounds like Coco and Luna were doing their jobs because you felt uncomfortable. It doesn't hurt Mr. Decker to learn to be aware of other people's space."

"A woman I used to know accused me of being too cranky; I told her she was too much of a busybody. When a mutual friend told me I had hurt the woman's feelings, I asked my friend if I was wrong. She laughed; I've always liked her."

Walt came into the office. "Hey, Wren. You doing okay, Aunt Jenna Lee? Nelson told me he was worried about your dogs because he said they were aggressive. He said he's worried they'll turn on you. Is something wrong with the puppies?"

Miss Jenna Lee snorted. "Nelson Decker is a..."

"Spineless letch," Wren added.

"My journalist is a wordsmith." Miss Jenna Lee's eyes twinkled as she smiled.

Walt glowered. "I'll tell Nelson to stay away from my fragile, elderly aunt and her sweet, killer puppies for his own safety; you let me know if he bothers you again, Aunt Jenna Lee."

After he left, Miss Jenna Lee said, "He's always been my favorite nephew."

"He's your only nephew, isn't he?" Wren asked.

Miss Jenna Lee tittered. "You're the smartest journalist I know."

Wren giggled as Tara came inside with Rascal, Coco, and Luna following her.

"I just had a royal greeting. Rascal and the puppies are so sweet. I wouldn't ask, but I need to know, what's funny?" Tara asked.

"Nelson Decker is a loser, but Walt is a keeper," Miss Jenna Lee said. "Did I say that right, Wren?"

"Perfectly."

"I don't disagree at all because I've had that same feeling," Tara said. "Do I get details?"

"Later." Miss Jenna Lee wiggled her fingers in a vague manner.

Tara raised her eyebrows at Wren, who nodded.

Tara set her briefcase on one of the chairs at the small table. "So, I've read the documents from the general contractor, and I don't have any problems at all with moving forward with his proposal. You can sign your approval anytime, as far as I'm concerned."

"I'll text Walt and let him know," Miss Jenna Lee said.

Wren glanced outside and bit her lip to keep from smiling. *Gage is lurking near one of the work trucks.*

"Is it okay if we raid your refrigerator for water, Miss Jenna Lee?" Wren asked.

Miss Jenna Lee nodded while she sent her text.

Tara joined Wren in the small storage room where the new refrigerator had been installed.

"Did you see Gage outside?" Tara whispered. "He was supposed to stay away."

"I'm not sure he can." Wren shrugged.

Tara narrowed her eyes. "What's that supposed to mean?"

Wren sighed. "You asked. I told him I was supposed to slit his throat."

"You what?"

Wren nodded. "He laughed and said maybe there's hope for him yet."

Tara left the storage room.

Wren stared at the three bottles in her hand. *Maybe I've been around Miss Jenna Lee too much; I appear to have lost my filters.*

After she set the bottles of water on the table, Wren asked, "Are we ready for lunch?"

"How many sandwiches are in the sack?" Tara asked.

Wren emptied the sack. "Three."

"Care to split one with me, Wren? They look huge to me."

"That's a good idea; I've been stressing about how much I've been eating lately."

Tara picked up one of the remaining sandwiches then left the office with the sack and a bottle of water.

"Where's she going?" Miss Jenna Lee asked.

"I think she went to yell at Gage. Are you eating at the small table or your registration desk?"

"I think the registration desk because I'm still on the clock."

Wren took a sandwich and a bottle of water to Miss Jenna Lee; as she sat at the small table, Tara came back inside.

Tara joined Wren at the table and slid her index finger across her throat as she winked then opened her bottle of water.

Wren grabbed a napkin and dabbed at her mouth to stifle a giggle.

The three of them ate in silence until Miss Jenna Lee's phone buzzed a text.

"Walt and the contractor will be here in five minutes for me to sign the papers," Miss Jenna Lee said. "After the contractor leaves, I'd like to have a discussion with Walt and Gage about our next steps after the completion of this project. Will both of you stay for that?" Tara's eyes narrowed; Wren raised her eyebrows, then Tara exhaled.

"I guess we will," Tara said.

"Good. I need your financial insight, Tara; Wren, you have the knowledge of the amenities of other successful campgrounds. Notice that I've included Lonesome Trail Campground in the successful category. I've always believed that being positive helps."

Wren blinked as Tara cleared her throat then dabbed her mouth with her napkin.

Wren stared at the last large bite of her sandwich to keep from laughing then shoved it into her mouth.

After they ate, Tara collected their trash as Walt, Nelson, and the contractor came into the office; before Walt closed the door, Gage slipped inside but remained close to the door. Nelson stood alone in the middle of the room with his arms crossed. Walt and the contractor, who had a scruffy beard and moustache, approached the registration desk.

"Miss Navarro, I appreciate the opportunity to participate in a project that's going to inject new life into this small community." The contractor's booming voice filled the room; he beamed as Walt put the contract on the desk in front of Miss Jenna Lee.

"I've signed the contract, Aunt Jenna Lee; I'll show you where you'll need to sign," Walt said.

"All of this okay with you, Nelson?" Miss Jenna Lee asked.

"Yes, ma'am, it is." Nelson glanced at Walt who glared at him. Nelson slowly uncrossed his arms.

"Well, let's get down to business; Walt, show me where to sign."

While Miss Jenna Lee initialed the first four pages, Wren glanced at Gage just as he winked at Tara. Tara's mouth twitched into a small smile, then she turned away with her nose in the air.

Wren smiled. *She's having a terrible time staying mad at him.*

Tara side-glanced Gage, who peered with great seriousness at Miss Jenna Lee.

"I can't even see this fine print, are you sure we aren't selling all our dairy cows?" Miss Jenna Lee grumbled.

Walt chuckled. "There are a lot of things I don't know, Aunt Jenna Lee, but I'm pretty sure our dairy cows are safe."

After she signed the last page, the contractor stuck out his beefy hand. When Miss Jenna Lee extended her hand, he gently held it as they shook hands. "Thank you, Miss Navarro; we'll get to work right away."

He and Walt strode out of the office, and Nelson rushed out behind them.

Gage stood at the open door and watched. "Nelson is leaving." Gage whistled, and Rascal, Coco, and Luna dashed inside.

Wren refilled the pitcher with water and refilled the dogs' bowl. "This is really handy, Miss Jenna Lee. The dogs don't have to wait for me to take away their bowl, refill it, then splash water all over the floor on my way back."

"I'd like to see where they're starting on the project," Tara said.

"I can give you a tour, if you like," Gage said.

"Do you want to go too, Wren?" Tara asked.

"I'd like to, but I'm under a deadline. I have to get back to my article."

After Gage and Tara left, Miss Jenna Lee said, "That was kind of magical, wasn't it?"

"It was fun to watch, that's for sure," Wren said.

When she reached the door, Rascal was at her side, and the puppies' heads drooped.

"We'll be back later; y'all need a nap," Wren said.

Cora and Luna trotted to their large bed, and Miss Jenna Lee chuckled. "Smart."

On the way back to the camper, Wren said, "Thanks for coming with me. Mr. Navarro said I should stay close to you."

After Wren and Rascal were inside, Wren sat at her booth and opened her laptop while Rascal flopped down next to her and closed his eyes. By the time she had opened her laptop, Rascal was lightly snoring.

I think I'll write my own version with a young woman not related to the Navarros who saves a little girl when the child falls from the bridge into the pond.

Wren spent most of the afternoon revising and adding new details for her article. After she finished, she read her draft, editing and shifting sections around as she went through each page.

When she finished her editing, she leaned back. "This is really close. I'll send it to Betsy."

After she emailed the third revision to Betsy, she sent her a text. "I sent you draft three by email."

Betsy replied, "Will read on my way to the interview this evening."

Wren closed her laptop. "It's nice to have other eyes review what I've written, Rascal."

Wren's phone buzzed a text from Tara. "I still need to talk to Miss JL. Are you available to come to the office?"

"On my way."

"Let's go to the office, Rascal. Tara has something she wants to talk to Miss Jenna Lee about and wants us there."

When they went inside the office, Rascal lay down next to the small table. When Coco nudged him, and he didn't move, Wren said, "It's too hot to go outside right now; it will cool down in a bit."

Coco and Luna picked up their chew toys and laid next to Rascal. Tara stood next to Miss Jenna Lee's desk.

"Thanks for coming, Wren; both of us wanted you to hear whatever it is that Tara has."

"I went through all your accounts and came across a foundation, and the only document I found that referenced it was from thirty-five years ago, Miss Jenna Lee. There are three signatures on it: yours, Eric Decker, and George Turner, your former accountant."

"The donkey rescue foundation," Miss Jenna Lee said.

"Exactly. I found when it was established, and that it is funded by a regular withdrawal from your stock dividends, but I didn't find any records of the account where the funds are deposited, so I don't know how the funds are being managed or even what the current balance is. What can you tell me about it?" Tara asked.

"Ever since he was a kid, Walt talked about running a donkey rescue. I set up the foundation for him; it's in my will, although when we first set it up, George told me anytime I wanted to turn it over to Walt, I could sign the papers, and Walt would have all the money. I have started making additional deposits to the foundation. Actually, I sent checks to Eric Decker, Nelson's father, then after he died, Nelson, and he takes care of it for me."

"Where do you keep your copies of the receipts, statements, your will, you know, things like that?" Wren asked.

"I keep them at home in my safe; Nelson dropped this month's off with me, but I haven't had a chance to take it home yet."

"That's understandable; it would be more comfortable for you to read your monthly reports at home."

Miss Jenna Lee chuckled. "I actually just file it. George told me I had access to all the electronic records and gave me access codes, but I had problems with the code and didn't want to bother him. It didn't matter because George or more often, Eric, and now Nelson, were good about taking me to lunch and updating me every month. Eric told me the monthly report that George prepared for us was much easier to understand than the detailed report, so that's what we always went over; Nelson did the same."

"Do you mind if Tara takes a quick look at this month's detailed documents from George's office? It might help her to understand the foundation better," Wren said.

"Not at all." Miss Jenna Lee pulled out a thick manila envelope and opened it with a sharp letter opener that resembled a small sword.

While Tara pulled out the first few sheets of paper, Wren said, "That's a really cool letter opener."

Miss Jenna Lee beamed. "It was a present from Eric when we set up the foundation."

As Tara glanced through the papers, she said, "This is really interesting and very helpful. Do you mind if I take it with me, so I can study the information here? I'll return the papers on Monday."

"Do you want me to bring the rest of the papers with me tomorrow?" Miss Jenna Lee asked.

"Why don't you leave them in your safe for now? I might want all of this year's records, but it will take me a while to go through this month's data," Tara said.

"I just had a thought." Wren cocked her head. "Who has your power of attorney?"

"Maybe Nelson, but I'm not sure I have a power of attorney."

"Is there a reason Walt shouldn't have your power of attorney?" Wren asked.

"Hadn't thought of that; after Eric died, Nelson and I revised my will and the papers for the foundation, and left everything the same except for the change to Nelson as my lawyer, but it makes sense now, doesn't it?"

"Does to me; do you have a copy of your will?" Wren asked.

Miss Jenna Lee snorted. "I'm certain I have a copy in my safe, but why would I need a copy? I know what it says: my will stipulates that everything goes to Walt."

"Is there anything I can do for you?" Tara asked.

"No, thanks for coming and not leaving any marks on Gage."

The puppies danced at the sound of Tara's musical laugh.

"Anytime. Let me know if anything else comes up," Tara said.

Wren and Rascal followed Tara to the door.

"Let's take a stroll to my camper, and we can talk," Wren said after she closed the door to the office.

On the way, Tara said, "The few pages I looked at were printed with a tiny sized font; I could barely make out the letters. Miss Jenna Lee couldn't have read what was on the pages with her eyesight, but it doesn't matter because it was Lorem ipsum: strings of letters as mockups of words to serve as placeholder text. I didn't find any receipts or records of any type for the foundation in the documents George's office sent me. I smell a rat or two. What was your take on her electronic records and access codes?"

"Miss Jenna Lee was probably too proud to admit accessing the records online was beyond her skills; she may even have asked for help, but accepted lunch as a substitute. They definitely took advantage of her weaknesses."

"The whole thing stinks."

"I'm concerned about her safety; Miss Jenna Lee needs a new will as soon as possible," Wren said.

"True, and I need to call for an audit immediately before I can sign on as her accountant; as far as a will is concerned, I know a lawyer in Waco, and she's good."

"Maybe Walt can take Miss Jenna Lee shopping in Waco. Rascal and I can take care of the puppies," Wren said. "I can run the office, or Gage can."

"We need Gage in on this." Tara pulled out her phone and sent a text. Gage raced to Wren's camper in the golf cart from the back of the campground.

"I was almost home when I got your text. What's up, Tara?"

"The three of us need to talk."

"Jump in; we'll go to my house," Gage said.

"Give me a second; I want to grab my computer and a notebook," Wren said.

After she came out of her camper with her laptop and backpack, Wren climbed into the back seat of the golf cart.

"Does Rascal want to ride?" Gage asked.

"No, he'll run along behind or in front if you're too slow."

Gage followed Rascal to his house.

"It wasn't a fair race, Rascal; I had two delicate passengers." Gage parked the golf cart in front of his house.

Tara glared at Gage; he clutched his chest and winced. "Ouch."

After they went into the house, Wren and Tara gazed at the high beamed ceilings, the cabin-style paneling on the walls, the substantial river rock fireplace and hearth with the large tin star over the mantel, and the three overstuffed sofas that were graced with bulky sofa pillows and were in a U-shape around an impressive glass-top coffee table. Western-style blankets of black, red, and gray were draped over the sofas. A wagon wheel chandelier hung over the coffee table. "This is gorgeous, Gage," Tara said.

"Thanks, but I can't take the credit; Mom had free rein. I only asked that she didn't do anything frilly."

"She's good; there isn't one frilly in sight," Wren said.

"Do you want to sit in here or at the table in the kitchen."

"I want to see the kitchen, but I don't care where we sit," Tara said.

When they walked into the kitchen, Wren smiled at the large wooden table with a wooden bench seat on one side and hand-hewn wooden chairs on the other side. Tara sat at one end, Wren sat on the bench next to her, and Gage sat across from Wren. Rascal flopped down in front of the old cast iron stove.

Tara told Gage about their conversation with Miss Jenna Lee. His eyes narrowed then his face grew hard. "I've never liked that jerk," he growled.

"We think Miss Jenna Lee needs a new will immediately," Wren said. "Do you suppose Walt could take her shopping in Waco tomorrow?"

"I have a friend in Waco who is a highly respected lawyer; I could give her a call and fill her in on our fears," Tara said. "She'll make time tomorrow for a new will and an appropriate power of attorney and have it ready immediately. It would be boilerplate, but right now, that's okay."

"Won't it look like Dad kidnapped Aunt Jenna Lee or something?" Gage asked.

"I don't think so at all, but if you're concerned, I'll go with them to the lawyer's office," Tara said.

Gage furrowed his brow. "You'll eventually be her accountant."

"Maybe, but if that's an issue, we can find a separate accountant for the foundation if it exists, and there's anything left."

Gage nodded. "Good point. I'll see if I can get Dad to break away from the construction, so we can fill him in."

Gage sent a text. "While we wait, how about cookies from the gas station and sweet tea or coffee?"

"I would love some sweet tea and gas station cookies," Wren said.

"So would I; I love coffee, but Miss Jenna Lee's coffee has coffeed me out," Tara said.

Wren frowned. "Is there any reason for Nelson Decker to be at the campground?"

"No, his only role was to review the contract, and he did that. His signature and approval aren't necessary for any of the construction," Gage said. "What are you thinking?"

"If he has power of attorney, would he have the right to oversee any of it?" Wren asked.

"No because the campground belongs to Dad and me, not Aunt Jenna Lee."

"What about the house? Is it part of the campground property because it's very well maintained."

"When we bought the property, the house had good bones, so the only updates it needed were cosmetic. The chandelier and furniture are all new except for that fine old stove and the tubs. The floors, walls, and the fireplace needed a few repairs and cleaning, but that was all. There is still a little more work to be done on the two bedrooms upstairs, but it's cosmetic, and Mom is working on that. The upgrades to the campground are more extensive and require more permits and inspections."

"Thanks, I always thought I was a pretty good journalist, but Miss Jenna Lee informed me that I was one nosy girl, so I've embraced my new role in life."

Gage and Tara laughed.

Walt walked in. "This can't be good if you two are not only in the same room but are laughing. Wren, blink twice if I'm about to be kidnapped by aliens."

Wren laughed. "That is so tempting, but sorry, no blinking."

Walt poured himself a glass of sweet tea and grabbed three cookies before he sat next to Wren.

He leaned close and whispered, "Elbow me if we need to make a fast getaway."

Wren rolled her eyes and held up a thumb.

"So, why am I here?" Walt asked.

Tara repeated the conversation with Miss Jenna Lee, and Wren filled in the rest.

"Don't you think a new will and a power of attorney is a little extreme?" Walt asked.

"Maybe, but we're worried about Miss Jenna Lee, so humor us," Tara said.

"What do you think, Gage?" Walt asked.

"I'm completely onboard, Dad."

Walt reached for the last cookie on the plate, but Tara snatched it away and took a big bite. Walt frowned. "That was my cookie; does anyone think this Donkey Rescue Foundation is real?"

Wren stared at him then picked up her laptop from the bench seat and set her it on the table. Gage pulled out another box of cookies from his pantry and set the box on the table. Walt slid the box in front of himself and out of Tara's reach. Tara glared at him.

Wren glanced up from her screen. *The cookie war is on.*

After several searches, Wren said, "It might be."

She turned her laptop to show Walt.

"Son of a gun; that's interesting. How do we wrestle away Aunt Jenna Lee's foundation from Nelson Decker's clutches?" Walt asked.

"I'll tackle that for a cookie," Tara said.

Walt removed two cookies then pushed the box to her.

Walt shoved a cookie into his mouth then asked, "Next question: who is going to tell Aunt Jenna Lee that she has to go to Waco with me and why we're going?"

Tara and Gage said in unison, "Wren."

"You're putting me in the middle," Wren growled.

"Better than throwing you under the bus," Gage said.

"About the same," Wren grumbled.

"Good, then you'll do it," Gage said.

"What time do I tell her to be ready to go?" Wren sighed.

"Tell her eight o'clock because she'll want to stop at the diner for breakfast," Walt said. "Tell her I'll take her out to lunch at her favorite place in Waco. She'd go then even if you told her I was taking her there for her first tattoo."

Gage spewed his tea. "Dang it, Dad. Give a guy a warning when you're about to say something so hilariously funny."

Tara laughed as she picked up the roll of paper towels from the counter and handed them to Gage. "Just hang onto these; your dad is always cracking jokes."

Before Wren closed her laptop, Tara said, "Send me that link to the Donkey Rescue that you found, Wren."

Wren sent the link then closed her laptop. "Unless there's anything else, I think it's time to chat with the woman who tells all she knows to let her know she has a road trip tomorrow, and she can't tell anybody. Walt, you'll have to explain why after you're on the road because Miss Jenna Lee has no filters. Wait, yes, she does. Never mind; I'll handle it. Come on, Tara; let's go."

Tara giggled. "You meant Rascal."

"Nope, he'll come with us; let's go."

"This was not the deal; not the plan at all." Tara pouted.

"No whining; I need moral support, and I'm tired of being by myself in the middle of something that is absolutely none of my business."

"Well, if you're going to be logical, then fine; besides, I'll get a ringside seat. So there, Gage," Tara said.

"What did I do?" Gage asked as Wren, Tara, and Rascal headed out of the kitchen.

"Just go with the flow," Walt said. "It's safer."

On the way to the laundry building, Tara asked, "Can we go to your camper first? I'd like to get everything lined up with my friend."

"Good idea; let's go."

After they were in the camper, Wren plugged in her laptop while Tara made her call.

Wren checked her email and wrinkled her nose when she saw a new email from Charlie. She quietly closed her laptop. *Later, Charlie.*

"We're set for tomorrow," Tara said.

As they strolled to the laundry room, Tara asked, "How are you going to convince her to keep going to Waco quiet?"

Chapter Nine

"What's the number one thing Miss Jenna Lee never talks about?"

"Herself."

"That's it; next question: why?"

"She absolutely likes to be in control; so, you're going to spin this as all about her, so she'll be in control? Seems simple, except I couldn't do it."

Wren nodded. "Just follow my lead."

"You have no idea what you're going to say, do you?"

"Nope."

Rascal dashed ahead; when they arrived at the laundry building, Rascal, Coco, and Luna waited for them in the shade. When Rascal gave a yip, the puppies dashed toward the campground; he grinned then raced after them.

"I've never gotten to know a dog as well as I know Rascal; he's amazing," Tara said as they went inside.

Miss Jenna Lee smiled. "Coco and Luna told me they desperately had to go outside; how's everything?"

"Everybody's happy to get busy with the construction. I don't know what their schedule is, but I'll bet they beat it," Wren said. "We did get asked a little favor though."

"Really? Care for some coffee or cold water? Is there anything I can do to help?"

"Cold water sounds good; I'll fetch," Tara said.

"Maybe, I don't know; I haven't figured out what we can do." Wren furrowed her brow as she waited until Tara handed out the bottles of water.

Wren moved closer to the registration desk and glanced around before she spoke quietly.

"The general contractor asked Gage if there was any way to occupy Walt tomorrow for most of the day. Evidently, Walt's trying to stay involved, and I guess that's fine, but the guys are worried about him wandering around while they're operating their heavy machinery."

"I wouldn't mind if Walt took me to lunch, but that's only part of the day, and who would watch the desk?"

Wren nodded, and Tara copied her as they furrowed their brows and sipped their water.

Miss Jenna Lee held up her index finger. "There's one option: Gage taught me this whole registration system; it took us almost a week, but I finally got it. We could keep him out of the way too, if he filled in for me while Walt and I were at lunch."

"That's a great idea; so, where is your most favorite place for lunch?" Wren asked.

Miss Jenna Lee snorted. "That's easy; there's a quaint café in downtown Waco that I adore."

"Really? What is it? Could I crash the luncheon and join you?" Tara asked. "I have a quick meeting with a client in Waco tomorrow."

"That would be fun. What about you, Wren? Would you like to go too?"

"I really would, but I'm feeling the deadline crunch for my article. I have another email from Charlie, but I haven't opened it yet; I honestly don't know what to do about that annoying man. He reminds me of Nelson Decker."

"That's easy. Dump him," Miss Jenna Lee said.

Wren raised her eyebrows and nodded. "You know, I think that's a fantastic idea. I'll finish up the article tomorrow and send him my resignation."

Tara narrowed her eyes. "No one should have to work with someone who is unreasonable."

Miss Jenna Lee gazed at Tara. "I wouldn't mind dumping Nelson Decker."

"I have a close friend in Waco who is an excellent lawyer, except she's young. Some people have a problem with that," Tara sighed.

Miss Jenna Lee snorted. "Their loss." She furrowed her brow. "Does she do wills? Do you think she'd take on a new client?"

Tara smiled. "That's her specialty; I could give her a call."

"Let's do that; see if we can drop in tomorrow sometime before or after lunch. We'll keep ole Walt busy the entire day." Miss Jenna Lee tittered. "I haven't had my nails done in ages; maybe we could do that too."

"That's perfect; I'll see if I can juggle my schedule and join you," Tara said.

Miss Jenna Lee chuckled. "We'll let Walt go to a hardware store."

"That's brilliant; that will definitely keep him happy."

"I'll give my friend a quick call to be sure she'll have time for us tomorrow." Tara went outside.

"I'm really sorry you can't go, Wren," Miss Jenna Lee said.

"I am too, but getting my article finished and Charlie out of my hair will remove a lot of stress."

"I feel the same way about Nelson Decker, but I wouldn't want that to get around."

"That's right; it's nobody's business but yours."

"Would you talk to Walt for me?" Miss Jenna Lee side-glanced Wren.

"His feelings might be hurt if he didn't hear it from you."

"You're right; I need to ask Gage to fill in for me tomorrow anyway. I'll talk to both of them at the same time."

Miss Jenna Lee furrowed her brow as she watched the puppies sleeping. "I worried about what to do with the puppies in the morning, then I remembered that the new groomer will pick them up at my house early tomorrow morning for their weekly baths and brushing. She'll drop them off here later in the morning; Gage can watch them. Everything's going to work out just fine."

Tara came inside. "We are set for a meeting tomorrow at ten; I'll meet you and Walt there." Tara put a slip of paper from her notebook on the desk. "This is her name, address, and phone number. The name under the phone number is her paralegal."

Miss Jenna Lee carefully folded the paper. "I'll give this to Walt in the morning. Ten is perfect because Walt can pick me up a little before eight, and we can go to the Whistle Stop for breakfast before we leave."

Miss Jenna Lee picked up her phone and sent a text then sent a second text. "I sent both of them a text asking them to come here for a short conversation. You two might want to skedaddle."

"I'll see you in the morning." Tara waved as she opened the door.

Rascal, Coco, and Luna rushed into the office; the puppies raced to their water bowl.

"Let's go, Rascal; you can have some water and collapse for the rest of the afternoon," Wren said.

Tara walked with Wren to her camper. "I'm still not sure how all that happened. It's like Miss Jenna Lee took over as soon as you told her there was a problem." Tara giggled then mimicked Miss Jenna Lee as she held up her index finger. "Control."

Wren's phone rang. "It's Gage."

Wren answered. "I have you on speakerphone, so Tara can hear."

"Hey, I've got you on speakerphone too, so Dad can hear. We both got a text from Aunt Jenna Lee. Is this an ambush?"

"In a way; she's going to ask you to take care of the office tomorrow while Walt takes her to Waco to see a lawyer for a new will. She has the name and address, and the appointment is at ten. You can't let her know we told you because this was all her idea," Wren said.

"With Wren's help," Tara added.

"Got it," Gage said. "We'd like details sometime, though. I'd like to learn from the master." Gage hung up.

Tara said, "I can't think of anything else we can do, so I'm heading home. Let me know if there are any changes."

"Sure will; keep me posted tomorrow."

After Tara left, Wren sat down at her computer to write.

Two hours later, Wren stretched. "I got lost in 'High Falutin' Killers'. Miranda's story was a good basis for an old-fashioned mystery."

Wren stomach rumbled. "Are you ready for supper, Rascal? I wouldn't mind more barbecue with extra burnt ends; we'll go to the gas station after you eat."

On the way, Wren's phone rang. "I hope that isn't Justin."

After she parked at the gas station, she looked at her phone and rolled her eyes. "I have a voice message from my illustrious publisher. I guess I should listen and most likely call him back."

She listened to the message. "Call me as soon as you can. We have a new wrinkle. This is Charlie. Bye."

She sighed then called Charlie.

"I was hoping I could catch you," he said. "Our editor wants to visit the haunted campground in Texas, but he's having trouble finding anywhere to stay; do you have any suggestions?"

"Waco is a little over an hour away, but he should check before he books the flight or a hotel because a large tornado traveled across central Texas yesterday and left a lot of devastation; there are still large areas with no electricity and a lot of debris. We lost power in the area, so the utility trucks may have the hotels booked up. I haven't heard yet whether the roads are clear between here and Waco, but I could see what I can find out. The campground was directly in the tornado's path, but thankfully, my camper was one of the few that the tornado missed. Work crews with heavy equipment are working around the clock to clear the campground and other businesses in the area of the dangerous debris; for example, the registration office was reduced to rubble, so that's one part of the cleanup at the campground going on right now."

"Wow; I had no idea; he might not be able to get a rental car either," Charlie said. "Does this slow you down?"

"A little bit; I'll see if I can catch up. I hope to send you a draft by Monday."

"Sounds good to me; sorry I didn't know about the tornado. I only pay attention to the weather when we're in the middle of wildfire season." Charlie chuckled.

Wren rolled her eyes.

After they disconnected, Wren said, "At least I didn't resign."

Rascal grinned.

When Wren went inside the gas station, Harper asked, "How's the campground, Wren?"

"A mess, as I'm sure you can imagine."

"What about your trailer?" Harper gazed at Wren. "Do you need a place to stay? Me and Mom can make room for you."

Wren's eyes misted at the sweetness and concern in the cashier's voice. "The tornado skipped my trailer, but thank you so much for the kind offer. I appreciate you."

"You just let me know if you need anything; do you have electricity?"

"It was off for a while, but it's on now."

"Air conditioning is critical in this heat. You take care now, ya hear?"

"You too."

As Wren stood in line, she listened to the quiet conversations in the line.

"We're lucky our county didn't suffer any loss of life," an old man said. "We can rebuild and replace things."

Several other men murmured their agreement; Wren nodded along with others who were in line.

"All my cows came home after the tornado," another man said. "I was afraid I'd lost them all. They're right nervous, though, and sticking close to the barn."

Gage appeared next to her. "What's for dinner, Wren?"

"Aren't you cutting in line?"

"Not if I'm buying; come have dinner with Dad and me. We've invited the contractor and his wife too. They rented a house about thirty miles from here, so his commute to the jobsite wouldn't be bad. A couple of the guys that were staying at the campground lost their campers, so they have house guests."

Wren shook her head. "I don't want to bust in."

"If you aren't there, we'll talk about the project all night, and the contractor's wife will be bored silly. If you were there, you could tell us to cut it out and quit being jerks."

Wren giggled. "What a tempting offer; okay, we'll come. What time?"

"Looking at the line in front of us, I should be back in forty-five or so minutes."

"Okay, I'll see you then."

When Wren stepped out of the line, Gage asked, "You're leaving? You trust me to buy dinner on my own?"

"You're the one who told me about burnt ends; yep, I trust you."

The man behind Gage chuckled. "She got you there, Gage."

Gage nodded.

Wren hurried to her pickup. When she opened the door, Rascal whined.

"Gage is buying dinner; we'll go to his house to eat."

Rascal settled down on the backseat and closed his eyes.

After they returned to the camper, Wren reviewed the article she'd written and made a few changes.

"I think the ending's not bad, Rascal. Listen to what I wrote: 'Because new owners have rescued the campground, and it's being renovated for more families to visit, the ghostly sound of Zuri's roar is one of welcome, the little girl is laughing, and the train's whistle adds to the promise of a great visit at the Lonesome Trail Campground.' So that's it; does it sound like the campground would be fun to you?"

Rascal rose then padded to Wren and put his chin on her knee. Wren stroked his neck.

"I'll ask Gage or Walt to read it, so I can have their perspective; after all, the point is to encourage people to stay at the haunted campground." Wren furrowed her brow. "Should I take out the mention of ghostly sounds? I'm not sure it fits; I'll leave it in for now while I think about it. I'd like for Betsy to read it, but I don't want to overload her."

Wren's phone buzzed a text from Betsy. "Leaving in five minutes; send me something to read."

Wren chuckled as she emailed her latest version of the 'Lonesome Trails Haunted Campground' article to Betsy.

After she fed Rascal, she copied her latest article to a flash drive to take to Gage's house and dropped it into a pouch in her backpack.

She snatched up her phone when it buzzed a text then sighed. *I thought it was Justin.*

Gage: "I'm back. Bring Rascal."

She smiled. "You received a special invitation to Gage's house; let's go." She started to pick up her jacket then shook her head. "I won't need it; we aren't in the Arizona desert, unfortunately."

Gage waited on the porch. "It's nice to see you, Wren; you look nice."

Wren rolled her eyes. "Gage, I'm wearing the same thing I was wearing at the gas station, but thank you for being a polite host."

Gage wrinkled his nose. "It was kind of over the top, wasn't it? I was trying to be mannerly; I won't let it happen again."

As they walked into the house, Wren said, "If you're practicing for Tara, she'll hand you your head if you say anything like that."

"I've been a flirty lout for so many years that I'm not sure who I really am or how to talk to people."

"You can be flirty, just don't be a lout; I take it back: don't be flirty with Tara."

"She'd rip me apart?"

"In a heartbeat. Before we go inside, I wanted to tell you that I have a final draft of the article I wrote about the campground. I'm very cleverly calling it 'You Decide: Is The Lonesome Trail Campground Haunted?' I have a copy on a flash drive that I'd like for you to read before I send it to the publisher.

"That's awesome; I'd love to."

When they went into the house, the general contractor rose from the sofa that was facing the fireplace.

"Wren, it's good to see you again." His booming voice rattled the glass in the chandelier as he held out his hand.

Gage whispered, "Dan."

"You too, Dan."

Wren smiled as they shook hands. *He's holding my hand that's half the size of his like it's a butterfly.*

"Wren, this is my wife, Phyllis." Dan put his arm around a woman who had joined him; she barely reached the top of his armpit with her head.

"Call me Phyl, Wren." Phyl glanced at Rascal then raised her eyebrows at Wren while she offered her hand for Rascal to inspect.

"Rascal," Wren said.

"You are a handsome guy, Rascal."

Walt came into the living room from the kitchen. "We have beer, wine, water, and sweet tea."

"What kind of wine?" Phyl asked as she strolled with Dan to the kitchen.

"Gage likes to keep a variety," Walt said. "Come see if there is something you might like."

Phyl read the labels of the wine that was lined up on a side counter. "I've never had this red; I'd like to try it."

"Wren?" Walt raised his eyebrows.

"I'll take a splash of the wine Phyl picked," Wren said.

After Walt poured the wine, he opened a beer for Dan and one for himself while Gage put a few ice cubes into a glass then filled it with sweet tea.

Gage raised his glass. "Cheers."

While Dan and Walt discussed a construction issue, Wren and Phyl carried their wine glasses into the living room, and Gage followed them.

"I'm going to my office for a few minutes," Gage said. "I won't be long."

Wren smiled. "Thank you."

After Gage left, Phyl said, "I understand you're a journalist, Wren. Are you here on an assignment?"

Wren told her about the travel magazine and the theme of her assignment.

"How exciting. Is the Lonesome Trail Campground haunted?"

"It depends on what you want to believe," Wren smiled.

"I want to believe it's haunted, so it would be haunted for me, wouldn't it?"

Wren's eyes widened. "Exactly; that's exactly the spirit, no pun intended, that I'd like the article to have for people. Each person can interpret the article for themselves."

"And come to the campground to prove they're right?" Phyl asked.

"Exactly."

"Did you do the same style of article in Arizona?"

"No, the legend of the campground there was completely different."

"So, why would a reader want to go to their campground?"

"The heartwarming, Old West story takes place at the campground with a remarkable hero."

"Ah ha, so readers can go to the campground and be steeped in the Old West of Arizona with the hero," Phyl said. "When will the article be published?"

"According to the publisher, the electronic subscription version is available now, and the print magazine will be shipped next Monday."

Phyl smiled. "I'll have to read it, then I'll have to drag Dan to Arizona after his project here is completed. We have a fifth wheel, but I didn't want to stay at the campground because Dan would have never taken off any time from work to rejuvenate for the next day if we were on site."

Walt stood in the doorway. "Food's ready; come and get it."

Gage hurried into the living room from the office and chuckled. "We run a classy joint."

Phyl and Wren strolled into the kitchen together. Phyl and Wren stopped and stared at the tall, muscular Dan with a white tea towel draped over his arm. "Our buffet is on the counter. Grab yourself a plate and fill 'er up," Dan said.

Phyl burst out laughing. "You look like a fancy maître d', sweetheart, but you sound like you fell off the chuck wagon."

"Thank you, my dear." Dan bowed.

Phyl snort-laughed, and Dan grinned.

Phyl picked up a plate and served herself as Wren followed her.

"Silverware's on the table," Dan said. "What would you like to drink with your meal?"

"Sweet tea," Phyl said.

"Same for me," Wren said.

"Psst. Rascal," Walt whispered; Rascal trotted to Walt.

Wren watched as Walt slipped Rascal two generous pieces of barbecue. Rascal smacked his lips and stayed close to Walt.

While they ate, Wren's phone buzzed a text. She glanced at it. "I apologize, but may I be excused?"

"Go right ahead," Phyl said. "I'll guard your food."

Rascal followed Wren as she hurried to the living room and read the text from Justin. "We're in Tucson. Do you have time for a call?"

Wren called Justin.

"Hi, honey; we made better time than we expected. We're already in Tucson, but we're thirty minutes early. We're in a line for ice cream."

"It was my idea," Betsy said.

"Tell her I knew that."

"I'll put you on speakerphone," Justin chuckled.

"I'm not surprised. Where's the meeting? At the school?"

"No, we're meeting at a coffee shop that doesn't have any ice cream," Justin said.

"Terrible faux pas on my part," Betsy said.

"How long do you expect the interview to be?" Wren asked.

"No more than an hour," Justin said. "A little shorter would be nice, but we have two major types of questions from our group: must ask and nice to ask, so it depends. We're next up at the pickup window. Talk to you later." Justin disconnected.

"Everything okay?" Gage strolled into the living room.

"Everything is fine."

"Are you sure?" Gage gazed at her.

"I'm positive; I'm just a little homesick."

"I read the article, and it blew me away. How do I get a reservation at that campground because I need to decide if it's haunted or not." Gage grinned.

Wren giggled. "Thank you; with your permission, I'll send it to the publisher."

"It's ready; do you mind if I let Dad read it tonight? He'll get a kick out of it."

"That would be great; just let me know if he has any reservations about it being published."

Gage laughed. "Reservations."

As they strolled to the kitchen, Gage asked, "How many more haunted campgrounds do you have to visit? When do you expect to complete your assignment?"

"Two more campgrounds, so I have no more than a month before I'm finished."

"That's not too bad, but that's easy for me to say," Gage smiled.

Wren returned his smile. "You're doing a good job of being a nice human."

Gage laughed. "Thanks; I think I'm not trying quite so hard to impress."

"That must be it. How well do you know Nelson Decker?" Wren asked.

"He was one of Dad's classmates, so I don't know him very well. Dad told me once that he was never impressed by Nelson because he always had a chip on his shoulder, but he said it was important to not let our feelings get in the way of being civil to people."

"That sounds like your dad."

"After we finish eating, I have dessert," Gage said as they went into the kitchen.

"I was counting on it, so I'm saving room."

"What were you saving room for?" Phyl asked.

"Dessert."

Phyl smiled as she looked at Dan; he returned her smile. "Our boys always said they always had room for dessert because they had a special pocket in their bellies where only dessert would fit."

Wren smiled. *That's The Look.*

After Wren helped Gage clear the dishes, Walt asked, "Have you ever heard of Texas sheet cake, Wren?"

Wren cocked her head. "No, is that what we're having?"

"I hope so because that's my favorite," Phyl said.

Walt served the four-inch by three-inch pieces of single-layer chocolate cake with a chocolate and pecan frosting that oozed over the sides of the cake onto paper plates while Gage poured five glasses of milk.

Walt said, "It's tradition at our house to have Texas sheet cake on paper plates, Wren."

Phyl laughed. "Ours too; it doesn't taste right, otherwise."

"Milk is important because it helps cut the sweetness," Dan added.

Wren took her first bite. "Wow, this is really chocolatey; I love it."

After Wren ate half of her cake and drank a third of her milk, she exhaled and stared at the cake still left on her plate. "I think I'll have either a bedtime snack or cake for breakfast."

Dan chuckled. "You wouldn't be the first for either of those choices."

After Gage wrapped her cake for her, Wren said, "This was wonderful; thank you so much for inviting me, Gage."

Before Wren left, Phyl hugged her. "We'll see you again. I'll let you know when I've read your Arizona article. I can't wait."

"I'll give you a ride, Wren," Gage said.

On the way back, Gage said, "Let me know if anything seems off or makes you nervous tonight, Wren. This whole thing with Raleigh Baker and now Nelson Decker has me nervous."

"I understand, but I'm not worried about myself; I have Rascal."

Gage nodded as he parked in front of Wren's camper where Rascal waited.

"I'll wait until you're inside; thanks again for your company." Gage grinned. "I'd say delightful company, but you'd punch me, wouldn't you?"

"I'm far too delicate to do anything like that." Wren giggled as she climbed out of the golf cart.

After she and Rascal were inside the camper, Wren said, "It was a pleasant evening, wasn't it?" She frowned. "I wonder if it's okay to freeze my
cake; I'll check."

When she turned on her computer, she moaned. "Another email from
Charlie."

She smiled as she read about freezing Texas sheet cake. "It will stay
fresher than if I just refrigerated it for a few days; perfect."

After she double wrapped her cake and put it into her small freezer,
Justin called.

"Hi, honey; tell me about your day."

Wren furrowed her brow. *Miss Jenna Lee's lawyer is a crook; we've found
her a new lawyer; she'll have a new will with her nephew as the main
beneficiary; I love burnt ends and Texas sheet cake.*

"I had dinner tonight with the campground owners, their son, the general contractor, and his wife. I officially love burnt ends and Texas sheet
cake."

"Texas sheet cake? I've never eaten it, but I hear it is super sweet."

"According to the contractor, milk cuts the sweetness. I think he was
probably right, but I could eat only half of my piece. How was the interview?"

"I'm actually pleased with the way the interview went. Betsy and I liked
the teacher; she'd be great for the school, but we brought up the commute.
I believe she has had concerns that she has been trying to ignore. She may
come to the conclusion that Hidden Gulch isn't right for her. Betsy and
I talked about it on the way back. Betsy's going to write up our findings,
then I'll review them. We intend to recommend her."

Wren furrowed her brow. "You're going to recommend her even though
she may leave after a year or two?"

"We decided we would; we don't have a crystal ball, so we don't know when she'd leave or if she might retire from our school system in twenty or thirty years. Betsy and I decided the commuting decision was the teacher's. Betsy's point was if anyone disagreed, they were welcome to fire us from the committee."

Wren giggled. "Very admirable."

"How's the article?"

"I'm happy with it; I shared it with one of the owners tonight, and he liked it. He'll have his dad read it; if he likes it too, I'll send it to Charlie."

"Any Charlie problems?"

"No more than usual."

"Do you know where your next campground is yet?"

"East of here; that's all I've heard so far."

"I hate that. It's farther away."

I agree. "In distance, but not in time. I have to tell you that I saw The Look tonight between the general contractor and his wife." She told him the story about the pocket reserved for dessert.

"Wren, I know you're giving me the sanitized version of your days; is that so I won't worry?"

Wren raised her eyebrows. *He's right.* "Of course, it is." She held her breath.

"Thought so. Do me a favor and cut it out; I can take it." Justin exhaled. "It's late in Texas; don't give me the edited version of your day tomorrow. In fact, why don't you catch me up on what your week has really been like tomorrow?"

"Are you sure that's what you want to hear?"

"No, but tell me anyway; it might not be as bad as I'm imagining."

Wren rolled her eyes. "Are you sure about that?"

"Should I stay up all night worrying about you?" Justin sighed.

"No, I have Rascal, so I'm safe."

After they hung up, Wren said, "One quick break, then what do you think about calling it a night, Rascal?"

Rascal yipped.

Chapter Ten

Wren woke when her phone buzzed; she groped for her phone in a groggy haze to turn off the alarm.

Rascal whined and put his face on her bed.

"I'm sorry; I don't know why I set the alarm to go off before daybreak."

She squinted at her phone. "It wasn't the alarm; I have a text from Gage at five thirty in the morning."

Wren read the text. "Call as soon as you're awake."

Wren called him.

"Wren, I just got a call from a friend of Tara's. She was in a crash yesterday on her way home and was airlifted to the trauma hospital in Dallas."

"Dallas?"

"It was the closest level one trauma center," Gage said. "I debated about texting you. If you can't go back to sleep, come have coffee with me."

"You have coffee? I'll be there as soon as I get dressed. Did her friend say what happened?"

"I'll pick you up." Gage hung up.

Wren quickly dressed and patted her holster in her waistband then measured and poured Rascal's breakfast into a plastic bag. "I'll feed you at Gage's house."

She picked up her laptop and grabbed her backpack. When she opened the door, Gage was waiting in the golf cart.

Rascal raced to Gage's house.

"What happened?" Wren asked.

"Coffee first; Dad's cooking breakfast for us."

"Do you have a bowl I could use for Rascal's breakfast?"

After Wren fed Rascal and sat at the kitchen table, Gage poured coffee then joined her while Walt put a platter of bacon on the table then began cracking eggs into a large bowl.

Gage glowered as he stared at his coffee. "Tara's friend said a large pickup with no license plates and darkly tinted windows signaled to pass Tara on the highway then rammed her car in the rear. Tara's car went into the ditch and rolled twice before it landed on its roof. The driver who was behind the truck immediately slammed on his brakes and jumped out of his car to help Tara. The truck that hit her also stopped as Tara crawled out of her car; when she tried to get up, she suddenly collapsed, and the truck sped away. When the driver who had stopped reached her, he discovered she'd been shot."

"Gage is leaving for the hospital, Wren." Walt finished scrambling the eggs he had in a large cast iron skillet. "If you don't mind staffing the registration desk, I can show you what to do before I leave to pick up Aunt Jenna Lee."

"Dad said I had to have breakfast before I left," Gage grumbled.

Walt put a large spoonful of scrambled eggs into Rascal's bowl. "Enjoy, boy."

He put the rest of the eggs on an oversized platter that was in the middle of the table before he pulled out biscuits from the oven.

"You made biscuits?" Wren asked.

Walt chuckled. "Impressive, isn't it? Actually, Gage keeps frozen biscuits in his freezer." He added a butter dish and a jar of homemade jam next to the biscuits.

"I can take care of registration." Wren placed a small serving of eggs and a slice of bacon on her plate.

Gage served himself eggs and bacon. "Thanks," he mumbled as shoved food into his mouth. He put his empty plate in the sink and grabbed a biscuit. "I'll let you know when I'm there, Dad."

Walt poured coffee into an insulated mug then handed it to Gage before he left.

While Wren buttered a biscuit then added a generous spoonful of jam to each half, Walt joined her.

"I read your article, Wren; it's very well done. You make the campground sound alive. I particularly like that the article didn't paint the campground as something it isn't: you know, too good to be true."

"Good; I didn't want anyone to show up and be disappointed because they expected something else."

Wren picked up her biscuit, and butter oozed over the side onto her hand.

Walt pointed to the paper towels in the middle of the table. "Now you know why they are there."

Wren giggled as she wiped her hand then took a bite of her biscuit. "Yum; this is really good."

"Glad you're enjoying it; Kendra canned a big batch of strawberry jam this last spring."

Wren furrowed her brow as she broke off a piece of bacon. "I'm not sure why Gage is going to the hospital."

"Before he left, Gage told me you'd be curious about that and gave me permission to explain to you. Gage and Tara used to date, and it was getting pretty serious until he pulled a stupid stunt and spent a drunken weekend with one of her so-called friends. You might have noticed he drank sweet tea while the rest of us had our beer and wine last night. His mother and I never dreamed he was an alcoholic." Walt shook his head in sorrow. "He's been clean for a long time now, but he never got over how he wrecked his chances with Tara. He was crazy about her then and still is."

"That's really sad; I knew there was some kind of connection between the two of them, but I didn't realize how deep it was."

"After we eat, I'll show you the computer system; it's not complicated at all. I'll let Dan know you'll need to know which sites have power. Before I leave to pick up Aunt Jenna Lee, you and I can check to see which sites are vacant. I doubt if we'll get any reservations, but you'll at least know what to do if we do. I hope you and Rascal don't get bored."

"You don't have to stick around to check the vacant sites; Rascal and I can do that. I'll have my laptop, so I can work while I'm there."

"Good; you can close for lunch and go to the diner to eat." Walt chuckled. "Aunt Jenna Lee's rule."

"Thanks." Wren smiled.

"We'll take the golf cart," Walt said as they went outside. "You'll need it later when you check the sites."

Rascal raced ahead of them and waited at the laundry room. Walt unlocked the door then gave Wren the key.

"I promise I'll take it back after we return." Walt grinned.

After five minutes of Walt showing her the reservation system, he said, "Aunt Jenna Lee doesn't know that we have system overrides, and that was not an oversight on our part, as I'm sure you can imagine."

After he explained the purpose of the overrides then pointed out how to activate each one, Wren said, "I understand how the overrides to issue partial refunds and to cancel incomplete reservations would be especially useful from a management perspective, but none of the overrides would be appropriate for Miss Jenna Lee."

Walt shook his head. "Not at all; she knows the standard processes, and any deviation would definitely not make sense to her. I'll drop off a thermos of coffee on my way out. I'm leaving a little early because if I left on time, I'd hear complaints the rest of the day about how tardy I had been my entire life and still am."

After Walt left, Wren set up her laptop on the small table then opened her email and sighed. "I'd forgotten all about the email I got from Charlie late last night, Rascal."

She opened the email, read it, and giggled. "I have to read this to you, Rascal; it's hilarious."

Wren cleared her throat then read in a somber voice. "The editor and I had a difficult but thoughtful discussion. We agree it would be wise if he doesn't attempt to visit the campground after all because of the unacceptable amount of unproductive time in airports and on planes. He sends his regrets and promises he will make an earnest attempt to visit with you at the next campground."

Wren laughed, and Rascal grinned. "I think we've figured out a way to handle that pesky editor: just threaten him with a trifle of inconvenience."

"I'll go over the article one more time later today then sit on it over the weekend to see if there are any additions that will beef it up a little; it seems a little short to me."

A little before the usual time the pickup trucks left the campground, Humberto came into the office; Rascal padded to greet him, and Humberto scratched Rascal's ear.

"Wren! I didn't expect to see you here; I went by your trailer, but you weren't there. I didn't think Miss Jenna Lee came in until ten, but I saw the light on and stopped by. Did she come in early?"

"No, I'm filling in until she gets here in case anyone requests a reservation, so I can contact them to let them know we're a little primitive for the time being."

Humberto nodded. "Primitive describes the campground perfectly right now. I came to talk to you because Tara was in a wreck last night. Did you hear?"

"A friend of the family contacted the Navarros."

"You know where she is then: a trauma hospital; don't mention it to anyone around here. One of the guys told me last night that a man was looking around for some muscle to teach a lawyer who was a broad a lesson."

"You think he was talking about Tara?"

"Yes; nobody likes lawyers, so it's not a surprise he found someone to do his dirty work; the guys would have laughed in his face and asked him what kind of sissy he was if he'd said he needed someone to take care of an accountant, even if they had no idea what an accountant was."

"I don't suppose anyone mentioned the man's name."

"No." Humberto narrowed his eyes. "I wouldn't be standing here if they did because I'd be in jail. One of my friends who was approached said he thought the man was a local because he was familiar with the campground and the road to Waco."

"Did he see the man?"

"No, the man told one of the new guys my friend is working with this week to ask around for someone to take care of a lawyer. I'll ask my friend to talk to the new guy; I gotta get to work. Keep my buddy, Rascal, close to you."

After Humberto left, Rascal grinned.

"You're getting the big head, aren't you? First the ghost tells me not everyone is what they seem, then the man in the store says the same thing and adds that I should keep you close; now, Humberto added his warning."

Wren furrowed her brow. "Not that I think it's a bad idea for you to stay close."

Wren reviewed the recent reservation requests to familiarize herself further with the system and found a reservation that had been made a week ago.

She stared at the screen. "Rascal, here's a registration for today that came in last week, but I don't see a confirmation or an assignment. I need to search for reservations today through next week."

After her search, she had a list of a dozen reservations for the upcoming week with no confirmations or site assignments. "I thought the confirmation was automatic." She checked the settings. *Automatic confirmations have been turned off.* She immediately turned them on.

When Walt came into the registration office with a thermos of coffee for Wren, she said, "I think Miss Jenna Lee may have been having trouble with the reservation system. We can go over them later, but she may be getting a little forgetful."

"Is there something you can show me?" Walt asked.

Wren showed him the screen with paid reservations but no confirmations. "The automatic reservation system was switched to manual; I found a dozen reservations for this upcoming week with no confirmations, so there are no site assignments; most of the people paid in full when they made the reservation. I have phone calls to make this morning, and I'll check the sites when it's lighter."

"I'll ask Aunt Jenna Lee how the reservations are going and let you know." Walt furrowed his brow. "She's always been very methodical. I can't see her inadvertently changing one of the defaults; she must have had a good reason."

Wren gazed at him. *He's making excuses, but he just needs time to think it over.*

"Make me a list of everything you find, and we can talk after I get back. I've already asked Dan to give you a list of the sites that are fully functional." Walt peered at the list of reservations. "If we don't have enough sites ready for this next week, let Dan know how many more you need."

"I will."

Walt shook his head. "This is a real mess on top of everything else. Text me if anything else comes up." He chuckled. "Or better yet, don't; I'll ask Kendra to clear her calendar, so she can take over the reservations. I'll have to come up for something for Aunt Jenna Lee, so she doesn't feel like we're dumping her." Walt exhaled. "I'd worry about you being here alone, but you've got Rascal, and Dan is onsite. Aunt Jenna Lee told me the groomer would bring the puppies here later this morning; I'd feel bad about everything we're piling on you, but Rascal will take care of the puppies, won't he?"

Walt waved as he left; Rascal grinned.

Wren poured herself a cup of coffee; while she made a list of people to call, she drank her coffee, and Rascal napped.

She wrinkled her nose. "I'll wait until nine before I call anyone. I can't tell whether anyone prefers a text because that's one of the options that was turned off."

Wren read through her article one last time. "It's as ready as it ever will be." She sent it to Charlie then scoured the reservation system for more automations that were turned off.

"Let's check sites, Rascal." Wren picked up a pad and paper for notes; she grumbled, "I wish I could print a map of the sites, so I could mark the sites on the map."

Wren drove the golf cart to the first row. She frowned as she scanned the sites. "They don't all have their site numbers anymore." She started a list of missing site numbers.

After she finished the first row, she exhaled. "This is taking a lot longer than I expected. I'll document the second row then make phone calls."

She finished the second row. "I need to find a site for the guests coming today. Their rig is big, so they probably have two air conditioners on their RV, and they're only staying one night, so they'll need extra length, especially if they're towing a car. The first row would be ideal, if any of the spots have electricity. I wish I had a multimeter; I could check myself." She exhaled. "I don't have to assign them a site right away; I've got time for Dan to check the sites, but I can still call them, confirm their reservation, and ask if they're towing and what time they expect to arrive."

After Wren called the first guest, she said, "Rascal, the good news is that they won't be here until after four, so I don't need to panic quite yet. They'll need a longer site because they're towing. They're traveling with a dog; should I point that out and make another pitch for the dog park?"

Wren looked through the folders on the computer and found the campground map and the campground rules. "I'll ask Walt if we can copy these two files to a flash drive and print a few copies. Campers expect them."

Rascal greeted Dan as he came into the registration office.

"Are you ready for a short walk, Wren?" Dan smiled. "Walt and I decided we should upgrade the entire campground to full hookups, so the large

RVs with two air conditioners can use any site, so we're about to make a big mess while we put in the utilities. Let's pick an area where the electrical system is adequate for the RVs you expect over the next two weeks."

As they strolled outside, Wren said, "It seems like the most convenient place would be the front row."

"That's logical except the first row's electrical system is toast. How many sites would you like to set aside?"

"It looks like we have about a dozen new reservations for the next two weeks; one of the RVs will arrive today."

"Assign it to the site farthest away from the registration building on the third row, so its way will be clear to leave in the morning; we'll tackle the first row today and should be able to finish it up by Monday."

"That should work," Wren said. "I don't think I should be making management decisions for the campground, though."

"Walt gave us carte blanche, so we could get started. I'll take credit for the brilliant decision if it makes you feel any better." Dan smiled.

Wren giggled. "Works for me."

After Wren returned to the office, the campground phone rang. Wren smiled as she thought about Betsy. *I love how she always answered the phone at the Forgotten Oasis Campground, but I'm not that brave.*

"Lonesome Trail Campground. This is Wren."

"I need to talk to Miss Jenna Lee," a man said.

Wren raised her eyebrows. *The man sounds like Nelson Decker.* "Miss Jenna Lee doesn't come into the office until later; can I help you, or would you care to leave a message?"

"What time will she be there?" he growled.

Wren glanced at the clock. *It's after ten.* "She's usually here by noon."

"Is she at home?" he asked.

Wren narrowed her eyes. *What business is it of yours?*

She replied in her frostiest voice possible, "I'm not at liberty to say. Is there a message?"

"There's something going on, and I have to talk to her about those reports," he shouted then hung up.

Wren snorted. *What was that all about?*

Wren's phone rang. *Gage!*

"I just got kicked out of Tara's room, so they could change the dressing on her wound," Gage said.

"You were in her room?" Wren asked. "How is she doing?"

"She had surgery last night to remove the bullet; the doctor said she was lucky that no vital organs were damaged. She has bruised ribs and a broken arm from the crash. Tara is exhausted from the whole ordeal, but she's talking to me in between her naps. I kind of fast-talked my way in, and she smiled when she saw me and didn't kick me out. She said she knew it was me when the nurse said her cousin was here to see her. Tara has a lot of cousins, and she knew it was me; isn't that amazing?" Gage lowered his voice. "I told her I was really scared, and she said she knew that."

"Are you going to stay there until she's released?"

"I'd like to, but Dad told me he wants Aunt Jenna Lee to retire, so I'll have to come back soon. I talked to Tara about it, and she understands. Her nurse told me the doctor would be more inclined to release her early if she had family to look after her. I told the nurse we would, so I've got my fingers crossed."

"Gage, you aren't her family."

"I've got plenty of room in my house for her; she can have my room, and I'll use one of the upstairs bedrooms. Wren, she'd be safe, but you're right; it's up to her and the doctor. I can go in now. Bye."

Wren smiled. *Gage knows how lucky he is that Tara is giving him a second chance; he knows it's his last one, but he'll be fine.*

Wren frowned. *I haven't heard from Justin today. Is he waiting to hear from me?*

Wren sent a text to Justin. "I sent in my final draft of the article. Now, I wait."

Justin replied, "Writing is easy for you. Waiting is tough."

"Call me tonight."

"Will do. Text any time."

Wren bit her lip. *He must be really busy.*

When the campground phone rang, Wren answered.

"Hey, Wren, this is Kendra Navarro. Walt told me that I need to learn the campground computer system. Aunt Jenna Lee doesn't know it yet, but she'll have a glorious retirement party, and I'm her replacement until the campground can get back on its feet, and we can hire staff. Walt said you could show me the reservation system and give me a list of improvements for it. If you don't mind, I'll bring lunch for the two of us today, so we can begin my first lesson."

"That sounds great; I look forward to meeting you."

"You too; see you later."

"I'm having lunch with Kendra Navarro, Rascal," Wren said.

Wren smiled at the sounds of heavy machinery outside and the beeps of the backup alarms. "I'll put in the site number for today's reservation, then I can write."

At eleven thirty, a young woman with curly, red hair piled in a topknot on her head came inside with Luna and Coco; the puppies swarmed Rascal then backed off when he yipped and scrambled to their water bowl. The young woman chuckled and knelt next to Rascal as she stroked his neck. "I've heard about you, Rascal. You're definitely an amazing puppy train-er."

The woman rose and headed to the door. "I turned over the puppies to Rascal, as ordered. I have to dash; it was nice to meet you, Wren."

"You too," Wren said as the young woman left. Wren shook her head. "I wonder what her name was."

A little after noon, a tall, slender woman who had short, gray hair and wore a bright green T-shirt, jeans, western boots, and dangling silver earrings shaped like spurs came into the office. She carried an insulated lunch bag and a large thermos. She set the bag and thermos on the small table then smiled as she extended her hand. "It's so nice to finally meet you, Wren, but I feel like I already know you. My husband and my son are captivated by your brilliance. Will I be allowed to read the article about the campground too?"

Wren returned the smile as they shook hands. "It's nice to meet you too. I have the article on my laptop; I'd love for you to read it."

"Excellent; let's eat first." Kendra pulled out two half sandwiches that were individually wrapped in plastic, small paper plates, paper napkins, plastic forks, and a covered plastic bowl and set them on the table. "We each have half of a chicken salad sandwich with a side of watermelon, and I brought sweet tea."

"What a perfect lunch." Wren picked up two plastic drinking glasses from the storage room before she joined Kendra at the table.

While they ate, Kendra asked, "Have you heard from Gage? I talked to him earlier this morning, and he said he was going to call you."

Wren nodded then dabbed at her mouth with a napkin. "I appreciated hearing that Tara is doing so well."

"He was adamant that he wanted Tara to stay here; it's probably a good idea from a security standpoint, but we'll have to see what Tara decides," Kendra said.

Wren giggled. "It will be interesting, won't it?"

"Exactly; it could go either way, but I don't think Tara is quite ready to trust Gage yet."

After they ate, Kendra said, "We should start with the computer system, shouldn't we?"

Wren shrugged. "Makes sense because after you take your break by reading the article, I'll bet you'll come up with questions. I know I did after I stepped away from it for a few minutes."

"Walt said you had some suggestions for improvements to the computer registration system."

"I do; I'm sure we'll come up with more as you and I go over it."

"Do you drive, or do I?" Kendra asked.

"Why don't you take the driver's seat? I'll talk you through the steps; that's how Walt taught me."

Chapter Eleven

After they went through the reservation system twice, including reviewing the overrides, Wren asked, "Ready for your break?"

"Durn tootin'." Kendra grinned.

Wren smiled as she opened her laptop to the article. "While you read, I'll take Rascal and the puppies outside. I want to keep an eye on them with the construction going on with all the heavy equipment; I'd worry about Coco and Luna because they are too small to see from the seats of those big machines."

"Great idea," Kendra mumbled as she read.

When Wren stepped outside, her eyes widened at the gaping trench across the camping sites on the first row. "Looks like more like dee-struction to me," she muttered.

Rascal led the puppies away from the campsites to the front parking area.

"Wow, they've already cleaned up all the debris from the office; with the temporary registration office set up, rebuilding the registration office can wait until after the new sites are added."

While Rascal, Luna, and Coco played, Wren glanced at a bulldozer as it lumbered toward the driveway.

She smiled. *Another critical improvement that won't take long but will add a lot of value. They sure aren't wasting any time.*

She watched the bulldozer as it roared away on the driveway to the road then listened as the bulldozer knocked down brush as it lumbered back to the campground.

"Let's see how Ms. Kendra is doing," Wren said.

Rascal led the way to the office, and Coco and Luna stayed close to him. Wren opened the door, and the puppies rushed to their water bowl.

"Wren, I absolutely loved the article you wrote. It was so refreshing to read a travel article that didn't make a location sound too good to be true. You made the campground sound inviting and a fun place to stay. Your writing talent is impressive."

Wren felt her face warm. "Thank you."

"So, tell me about your writing assignment; Walt said you'd be moving on soon."

"This was my second haunted campground to visit out of four. I've submitted my article to the publisher, who will let me know where I'm going next. I know it will be east."

"You've been here such a short amount of time, but you've had a big impact on my family; you can be sure we'll be watching your career and reading whatever you write. Do you plan to stick with writing articles for magazines?"

"Freelancing and writing articles is what I've done since I graduated from college, so it's comfortable for me. I've been writing some fiction while I've been here to entertain myself. I may look into that more seriously."

"If you need a beta reader, let me know. Mysteries are my favorite, which is why I think I love your article so much," Kendra said. "I'll have to be at the office full-time until we can afford to hire someone, so I'll have a lot of extra time on my hands. I've already told Walt he'll have to hire someone to clean the office and the restrooms and someone else for maintenance, mowing, and all the outside work."

"Thank you; I'll remember that."

"What's your cell number? I'll text you my email address." Kendra pulled out her phone.

After Kendra entered Wren's cell phone number and sent her text, she said, "I do have some questions about some of the automations that aren't turned on. I have a list; do you know what these do?" Kendra pointed to a sheet of paper next to the office computer.

Kendra and Wren went through each of the automation flows. After they finished, Kendra stretched. "We have only four left out of my original ten; not bad. I'll talk to Gage about those four."

When the campground phone rang, Kendra raised her eyebrows. "Should I be brave?"

"Do it," Wren said. "You can always hand the phone to me, and I'll make something up."

Kendra smiled. "I can do that." She picked up the phone. "Lonesome Trail Campground, how may I help you?"

Kendra raised her eyebrows. "I'm sorry, Miss Navarro is not available right now; how can we help you today?"

Kendra frowned as she listened.

"Are you a family member?" Kendra asked.

She pulled away the phone and stared at it before she set it on the desk.

"He asked me where Aunt Jenna Lee was; I didn't quite tell him it was none of his business, but he obviously got the point because he hung up; he was quite agitated that she wasn't available."

Wren frowned. "He's probably the same man who called earlier this morning; I loved what you said, by the way. I told him I was not at liberty to say when he asked where she was."

Kendra smiled. "Great minds think alike, don't they? I'm glad Walt decided Aunt Jenna Lee has to retire. I don't like the sound of this man, and I certainly wouldn't feel comfortable with her at the office by herself. I want to know who he is and what he wants. Do you have any idea?"

"Is it okay if I don't say anything right now?" Wren bit her lip.

Kendra narrowed her eyes. "Maybe I already know, and I agree with staying low key."

Wren exhaled. "Good."

Kendra nodded. "Let's talk about something else. I forgot to mention I brought cowboy cookies. Ready for an afternoon break?"

"I've never heard of cowboy cookies," Wren said.

"Oh my goodness, child; you've lived a sheltered life. They're oatmeal, chocolate chip, shredded sweet coconut, and toasted pecan cookies, but cowboy cookies is much quicker to say."

Kendra handed Wren a cookie.

Wren's eyes widened. "This cookie is huge."

"It wouldn't be a cowboy cookie if more than two of them can fit on a dinner plate," Kendra said.

Wren picked up her cookie and stared at it. When Kendra broke hers in half, Wren exhaled and copied her.

After Wren finished her half of a cookie, she sighed, "So good."

Kendra handed her a quart-sized plastic bag. "For later."

"Will you be okay by yourself? I thought I'd go back to my camper and write."

"Isn't your article finished?" Kendra asked.

"I never thought I could write fiction, but I've kind of challenged myself to write a mystery. It's a big change from writing a magazine article and has become my stress relief valve."

Wren slid her remaining half of the cookie into the plastic bag and put it into a pouch on her backpack then picked up her laptop. "Are you coming with me, Rascal?"

Rascal yipped at the puppies who whined then yipped as he trotted to the door.

Wren and Rascal were careful to stay clear of the heavy equipment as they hurried to Wren's camper. After they were inside, Wren said, "I told Kendra I was going to write, but I'm afraid I'm almost too exhausted to write. Maybe I'll write half an hour or so then take a break."

Rascal flopped down next to the sofa while Wren pulled down the shades then stretched out on her sofa with her laptop. She wrote until she her eyes burned then closed her laptop and put it on the floor.

"I'm not used to this much screen time," Wren said. "Let's sit outside and watch the construction progress."

When they were outside, Wren said, "I forgot my camping chairs and the picnic table were gone. We could go for a walk, but we can't walk around the campground, and I'd have to put on my gaiters to go for a walk in the woods. Let's check the driveway; they should have it wide enough by now for us to leave for the gas station."

When they reached the driveway, a huge pile of gravel blocked the exit as a bulldozer rumbled toward the pile to spread it on the driveway.

Wren crossed her arms as she watched the bulldozer. "Let's go back to the camper; I'll relax in the shade and sit on a step."

Rascal wandered around the camper while Wren wrestled with the awning. "This dang thing got twisted by the tornado. I can't get it to open."

Rascal leaned against her; Wren exhaled. "Why is everything suddenly so frustrating? Justin's too busy to even text; I haven't heard anything from Betsy, and there's nothing to do."

Rascal stared at her.

"I sound like I'm feeling sorry for myself, don't I?" Wren sat on the step and propped her elbows on her knees while she rested her chin on her palms.

Rascal flopped down next to her as she listened to the roar of the heavy machinery and the shouts around her. The constant noise droned around her, and Wren relaxed.

"Why do I think Justin has to text me? He tells me all the time, 'text or call anytime;' well, this is an any time, isn't it?"

She pulled out her phone then smiled as she tapped her text. "My life is exciting. My plan for today is laundry."

Justin responded. "Good clean fun is always exciting. Thanks for the update, honey."

Wren laughed. "He must be really busy, but he's not too busy to respond to a mundane text. I feel better, but since I am running out of clean clothes, let's do laundry and pester Kendra."

Rascal jumped up while Wren went inside and gathered her dirty clothes, detergent, and her pill bottles filled with quarters for the machines. He romped alongside her as she carried her basket of dirty clothes to the laundry room that doubled as the registration office.

When Wren opened the door, Rascal yipped, and Coco and Luna bounded to join him outside.

After Wren went inside, Kendra said, "I sure am glad to see you. Do you feel cooped up? The puppies and I took a short walk toward the front of the campground, and the driveway's blocked. I don't have anywhere to go, but I feel trapped."

"That must be my problem too; I'm really out of sorts today."

After Wren put her dirty clothes in the washer and fed the machine quarters, she asked, "Have you heard anything from Walt?"

"He's still in Waco; Aunt Jenna Lee decided to get her hair and nails done, so he's at his favorite sportsmen's mega store. He sent me a text with a photo of an all-terrain utility vehicle that he said is important to get as soon as possible for the maintenance jobs at the campground. Walt claimed the golf cart should be reserved for the office staff to show the guests how to get to their sites because it was bad customer service if the guests can't find their sites and go the wrong way. I'm not sure why I can't step outside the door and point, so I guess I have more to learn about running a campground."

"Miss Jenna Lee told me to drive around and find a spot that had electricity."

Kendra laughed. "That's terrible, and I apologize for laughing, but that is so typical of Aunt Jenna Lee. We'll have to have new campground maps made as soon as we can, won't we?"

"I found the old map and the campground information sheet on the office computer, except the sheet was more rules than information. Gage said he ordered a new printer, but it won't be delivered before next week."

"Did you read the rules? Is there anything there we can salvage?" Kendra asked.

"Maybe one or two things like quiet hours and the campground speed limit. I don't think they've been updated in ages because the sheet doesn't even mention wi-fi, and good internet access is critical for campers these days."

"The campground has wi-fi?"

"It did before the tornado, but now the office is using the wi-fi from Gage's house. He set it up almost the first thing after the tornado. I was surprised because I don't think of the marketing types as being techies."

"He's always been really talented in a lot of areas; I'm glad he's joined Walt in their campground venture because it presents greater challenges for him than marketing ever did. He thrives when he's solving problems in his own creative ways and is bored by routine."

"I can see that."

"So, what brought you here, other than dirty laundry and your kind heart that knew I was bored too?" Kendra smiled.

Wren giggled. "Was it that obvious that I was so bored that I decided to do laundry?"

"Well, I'm really glad you're here; we'll have to get this place profitable as fast as we can, so I won't be stuck in registration all day. I don't mind filling in, but I'd have to take up needlepoint, wood carving, or ax throwing to keep from falling asleep. I don't see how Aunt Jenna Lee has put up with it so long."

"Crossword puzzles." Wren gazed at Kendra. "I'm not sure I agree it's a good idea to retire Miss Jenna Lee."

"She does crossword puzzles? Really?" Kendra furrowed her brow. "Maybe I should tell Walt not to retire Aunt Jenna Lee after all; maybe she could be here in the mornings to staff the phones and be a presence, then I'd take over in the afternoons. Don't you think I could keep the registrations straight and make sure everyone had a site before they showed up in the afternoon?"

Wren smiled. "That has real possibilities; now, I see where Gage gets his creativity."

Kendra picked up her phone and tapped a quick text.

"I hope this works out," Kendra said. "Aunt Jenna Lee has never been one to stay home or be a part of the tea and gossip crowd."

"While I'm not minding my own business, have you noticed her eyesight is failing?"

"No, I haven't; we'll get her to a good eye doctor, so she can do her crossword puzzles." Kendra shook her head. "When I was pregnant with Gage, she told me I should always exercise every day, and words were the best exercise of all. I always I thought it was one of those Aunt Jenna Lee-isms."

Kendra's phone buzzed a text; she read it and smiled. "Walt hadn't mentioned retirement yet. I'll bet he's relieved because that would have been a hard conversation for him; he's very soft-hearted."

Wren moved her clothes from the washer to the dryer and fed quarters to the dryer then glanced at her phone. *Nothing. I should have brought my computer; I could be writing.*

Wren sighed.

"What?" Kendra asked.

"I was writing, but my eyes burned, so I quit to rest my eyes. Now I wish I had my computer, so I could write."

Kendra nodded. "And burn your eyes."

"Right." Wren giggled.

"They say you should look out a window every fifteen minutes to rest your eyes. Do you ever wonder who They are and why They make up all this stuff?" Kendra smirked.

"That was certainly worthy of being a Miss Jenna Lee-ism: sounds non-sensical, but with a world of truth behind it; I'll give the window thing a try," Wren said. Kendra pulled up the old site map on the computer. "Wren, I noticed something earlier. How closely have you looked at the old map?"

Wren joined Kendra and stared at the screen. "Maybe not close enough; what did you see?"

Kendra pointed. "This section with the sites in blue are probably the current sites, right?"

Wren peered at the screen and nodded. "But that's only a third of the sites on the map; there's a larger section of green sites next to the blue sites. If you glance at it quickly, they look like green trees, don't they?"

"I'll bet that's why they didn't click in your brain as sites."

"Make it larger," Wren said.

Kendra raised her hands and moved away from the keyboard. "You do it."

Wren nodded then made the map larger. "Each row of site numbers continues from blue through green."

"So, it looks like the campground was quite a bit larger, doesn't it?" Kendra asked.

"Did Walt have the campground surveyed when he bought it?" Wren asked.

"We can ask him, but I seem to remember that someone gave him a survey..." Kendra furrowed her brow. "I can't remember."

"Miss Jenna Lee told me the frontage property, for lack of a better word, was split in two by a speculator and sold in two parcels. What if that's true, but the original campground owner bought both parcels at different times? I can try to research it."

"Don't bother; I have a friend in the county assessor's office; she tends to be a know-it-all, which is really annoying because she's always right. Can you give me the parcel numbers or coordinates of both pieces of property?

I'll ask her to find the history of both parcels. Just to let you know, this is going to cost me a batch of cowboy cookies."

Wren emptied the dryer into her laundry basket. "Will she research the properties without letting anyone know who was asking?"

"I'd forgotten about Raleigh Baker and Tara: someone dangerous has something to hide." Kendra shuddered. "Yes, she's not one to brag about what she discovers, and it's what she does all day, so it won't even draw any attention to her."

Wren nodded as she hurried to the keyboard then wrote down the parcel numbers and the coordinates for each parcel; she stared at her notes then added the parcel number and coordinates for the additional section of property that she had discovered Miss Jenna Lee owned.

She pointed to her notes. "The first two parcel numbers and coordinates are the frontage property that are shown on the old campground map; the third one is the parcel number and coordinates for the property behind the old campground map where the old Lonesome Trail Railroad and Zoo might have been."

"I'll bet this will cost me two batches of cookies; if we can get Aunt Jenna Lee here tomorrow morning, you've been volunteered to help me make cowboy cookies."

"Volunteered?" Wren rolled her eyes.

"Of course." Kendra sniffed. "I volunteered you myself."

"Fair enough, but I'm not unpaid labor, right?"

"Of course not; you'll be paid a bounty in cookies, and yes, they are perfect for freezing."

"Okay, then just let me know what time to show up for cookie duty." Wren picked up her laundry basket and opened the door. Rascal, Coco, and Luna trotted from a nearby shade tree to the office; the puppies rushed inside, and Wren and Rascal hurried to their camper.

While Wren folded her clean clothes, Rascal took a long drink then scratched his rug as he turned in circles before he flopped down, closed his eyes, and immediately slipped into a soft snore.

After Wren picked up her laptop from the floor and put it on the massive table, she poured herself a large glass of sweet tea. She sat on the bench seat, opened her laptop, and groaned. *Email from Charlie.*

She sighed. *Okay, Charlie, ruin my day.*

She read the email. "I love the article; however, the editor is rightly concerned that it does not match your first article. This second article makes the reader want to go to the Lonesome Trail Campground to help the ghosts be happy again. Your first article invited the reader to share in the Old West experience of the Saloon Lady at the Forbidden Oasis Campground. According to the editor, this is too drastic a change for a series of articles. Please revise. As ever, Charlie."

"They understood the article; that's amazing."

Rascal peered at her through his sleepy eyes.

"I think I'll give good ole Charlie a Miss Jenna Lee reply, Rascal; what do you think?"

Rascal closed his eyes.

Wren peered at her screen then typed her reply. "I'm beyond thrilled that you and your editor understood the Forgotten Trail Campground article so well. Unless there are any grammatical errors, which I assume there are not since you didn't mention any, I won't be revising my article, which is final and ready for publishing."

"What do you think, Rascal? Is that clear enough?"

Rascal snuffled in his sleep.

After Wren sent her email, her phone buzzed a text from Gage.

Chapter Twelve

Wren shook her head as she read Gage's text. "Tara's mom is taking her home tomorrow morning. I'm on my way back."

I'll bet he's disappointed, but I agree with Tara.

She replied, "Sorry. See you later."

Her phone rang. *I'm getting more phone calls in the past few weeks than I got over the past five years. At least, my phone etiquette has improved.*

"Hello, Tara."

"Did you hear from Gage?"

"Yes, he said he's on his way back; I'm sure he's disappointed."

"He'll see the logic, or he won't; I'm willing to wait. I think I know why I was shot; do you?"

"No, not at all." *Why was Tara shot? Wrong question. Why was the accountant shot?* "Wait, yes. There must be something in Miss Jenna Lee's records as tiny as the print is, that would jump out at an accountant."

"My thoughts exactly; next question: what?"

"So, I get the files from Miss Jenna Lee's safe for you to review, which will most likely get both of us shot. Am I close?"

"Can you say that a different way?" Tara sighed.

"Sorry, it was kind of a cliché, wasn't it? Get both of us knocked off. Better?"

Tara giggled. "You're nuts, but I'm worse; yes, much better."

"So, that's why you kicked Gage to the proverbial curb: to get him away from the bull's eye."

"You don't know that, and you can't repeat it," Tara growled.

"You already got me knocked off; I'm impervious to threats."

"I still need the papers, so I can see why we're being bumped off."

"Okey, dokey."

"I think I can meet you somewhere close to you after you get the papers, so I can review them; I have an idea, so I'll work on that."

After they hung up, Wren sent a text to Walt. "Call when you have a few minutes."

Walt called immediately. "I'm sitting outside the beauty salon; Aunt Jenna Lee is supposedly ready to leave, so I probably have more than a few minutes. Whatcha got?"

"Miss Jenna Lee has all of her detailed monthly financial records in her safe. I need the past year's records; could you get them for me when you drop her off?"

"I'm sure I can. What's up?"

"I don't really know, but the print is too small for Miss Jenna Lee to read, so I'd like to see why."

"You're getting them for Tara, aren't you? I heard from Gage; he had his heart set on protecting Tara."

"I know; he texted me that he is on his way back."

"How did it go with the lawyer?"

"I liked her, and her paralegal is topnotch. The paralegal told me she'd file Aunt Jenna Lee's will with the county probate court today."

"I don't know anything about the process, but that sounds good to me."

Walt chuckled. "That was my reaction too. How's the work going at the campground?"

"I didn't realize the driveway to the campground was going to be widened, but that was really needed, wasn't it?"

"It's hard to believe it wasn't done long ago, isn't it? Dan and I talked early this morning and decided that we might as well widen it right away for the equipment we'll be bringing in, but it is definitely critical for the big rigs people use for camping these days."

"The last time Rascal and I checked, it looked like they were dumping gravel on it."

"The driveway will be closed for a couple of days for it to settle. If you haven't already found it, ask Dan to show you where the temporary entrance and the exit are. After the main entrance is drivable, Dan plans to make the temporary exit the permanent exit, so we won't have the big rigs passing each other. That was Dan's idea: he said some of the new RV drivers make him and his crews nervous. I think he already put up the sign for the temporary entrance on the road, but the exit may not be marked on the campground side yet."

"I didn't know the gravel needed to settle, thanks."

"Glory be; here's Aunt Jenna Lee. Let me know if anything else comes up. I'll let you know when we're at Aunt Jenna Lee's house."

After they hung up, Wren said, "There's a temporary exit; we can go to the gas station to look for a camping chair."

Wren called the office; when Kendra answered Wren said, "I just heard there's a temporary exit for the campground. Do you know where it is?"

"I didn't know they did that. I'll have Dan come to your camper and show you."

While Wren closed her computer in preparation for leaving, Kendra called.

"I just talked to Dan, Wren; the exit is on the other side of the camp-ground, which is no surprise, and they're putting up an exit sign right now, so you'll either see the sign or the workers putting it up. Where are you going?"

"Rascal and I are going to the gas station; my camping chairs blew away. Do you need anything?"

"I can't think of anything; I'll text you if I do. Is that okay?"

"That's just fine."

Wren headed toward the end of the row and spotted the temporary exit sign painted on a scrap sheet of plywood. As she drove toward the road, she said, "They really smoothed this out, didn't they, Rascal? I expected it to be much bumpier than this."

On the way to the gas station, Wren glanced at her gauges. "I have half a tank; I'll fill up while we're here."

While she waited behind a car at the gas pump, Wren narrowed her eyes as a car pulled in and parked in front of the store. *That's Nelson Decker.*

After she refueled, Wren parked several cars away from Decker's car. "It's too humid to wait in the truck, Rascal."

Rascal jumped out when she opened the back door for him, then the two of them headed toward the store.

Rascal sat near the door in the shade as Wren went inside.

Harper smiled and wiggled her fingers in a wave while she waited on a woman.

Wren smiled and princess-waved in return; when Harper giggled, the customer glanced at Wren and chuckled.

Wren headed to the camping section but slowed when she heard Nelson Decker's voice in the next aisle.

"I'm telling you I'm worried about Miss Jenna Lee: her eyesight is just about gone, and she's in a serious health decline, and I think someone's taking advantage of her. Walt doesn't seem to care all that much. She's been alone at home and is very vulnerable; he hasn't bothered to check on her once. Isn't that elder abuse? I have half a mind to report him."

"I think you're exaggerating like you always do, Nelson; you and your dad, rest his soul, have been her lawyers for years, but if you think there's something wrong, aren't you legally obligated to report it?" a woman asked.

"You're not a lawyer; where do you get off quoting law to me?" Nelson growled.

"Hey, hey, Nelson; settle down," a man said. "You're talking kind of rough to the lady there after she was polite enough to listen to you spout off."

Wren smiled. *He got you there, Nelson. Your move.*

"Mind your own business," Nelson muttered as he stomped to the front.

Nelson shouted, "There's a stray dog at the door; you need to call somebody."

"On it," Harper called out.

As Wren hurried to the front, Harper said, "Come on in, Rascal. I've got a special treat for you."

When Wren reached Harper, she glanced around. "Where's Rascal?"

Harper smiled. "Oh, he's back here with me. I gave him a treat for scaring away Mr. Decker, who is no longer welcome in the store unless he promises not to harass the other customers."

Rascal grinned when Wren peeked around the counter.

"Go do your shopping, Wren; we're fine here."

While Wren was in the camping section admiring the colored lights for awnings, a woman in the next aisle said, "Did you hear about Jenna Lee, Penny? She's deathly ill, and none of her family has been to see her."

Penny snorted. "You say that like you expected more from Walt, Nadine, but with a son like Gage..." Penny lowered her voice as she sneered, "The apple doesn't fall far from the tree, does it?"

Wren headed toward the aisle with fire in her eyes, but the man who helped her find her gaiters stepped in her path. "Let it go, Wren," he said quietly. "Nadine and Penny are known troublemakers, and nobody listens to them."

Wren exhaled. "It was such a blatant lie."

The man nodded. "If they said the sun was shining, everyone around them would grab an umbrella."

Wren giggled. "Thank you."

"You're a good friend to good folks, Wren; we're glad for the time you're here. Now, what are you looking for?"

"My camping chairs blew away; I need one, but I'd like to have two in case I have company."

"Let's look in the garden section; sometimes the obvious place to look isn't obvious at all."

Wren smiled as she followed the man. *Everything he says sounds like a rare gem of wisdom.*

When they reached the garden section, Wren slowed as she looked at the seed packets.

"Sunflowers are easy to grow from seeds, and they love hot weather," the man said. "Here are your camping chairs."

When Wren turned to look at the camping chairs, the man was gone. She picked up a seed packet of sunflowers before she selected a green chair then spotted a bright yellow chair that reminded her of sunflowers. After she paid for the chairs and packet of seeds, she and Rascal went outside. She put her chairs in the back of the pickup, Rascal jumped into the backseat, and she dropped her seed packet in her cupholder. She glanced at the sunflowers on the front of the seed packet and smiled as she headed toward the campground.

After she passed the old entrance to the campground, she saw the large sign that said 'Entrance' in gigantic letters with an arrow pointing toward the campground. The temporary entrance drive was as smooth as the exit and as wide as the new driveway.

After she parked next to her camper, she opened Rascal's door then pulled out the two chairs and set them in front of her camper. She stepped back and smiled. "We have sunflower chairs, Rascal."

Wren sat on her yellow chair while Rascal took a break then stood next to her. When Wren's phone rang, she said, "Yay, it's Betsy."

"Are you okay? I just heard about a tornado in Texas. Was that anywhere close to you?"

Wren smiled. "Rascal and I are fine; what's going on there?"

"Oh, nothing much," Betsy said.

Wren frowned. *Something's wrong.*

"Well, it's still hot, but I guess you probably knew that." Betsy cleared her throat. "Socorro's getting better. Butch sprained his ankle, but he's doing okay; he'd probably heal faster if he'd stay off it, but that's not going to happen. Well, guess I better go; I've got a lot of work to do."

Wren narrowed her eyes. "Really? That's too bad; so, what's wrong?"

"I didn't say anything was wrong; maybe not quite right, you know, a little off, but not wrong. Well, I'm glad the tornado wasn't close to you. Gotta go." Betsy hung up.

Wren called Socorro.

"Hey, Wren; I knew you'd call me. Betsy called you to ask about the tornado, didn't she? She's been stressing about that tornado all day."

"Yep, she did, so, what was it that she was trying to avoid telling me?"

"I knew you'd catch that. It's not up to me to tell you, but I'm telling you anyway because it is so ridiculous. Betsy's pretending not to be worried about the teacher candidate she and Justin interviewed yesterday afternoon. She told me she thought Justin and the candidate hit it off only too well for her liking. When I asked her for specifics, she said it was just a feeling. She's been moping around all day about it; Butch told me she's been distraught over a phone call she received earlier today and asked me to talk to her, and I did, but I got mad at her for listening to busybodies and yelled at her, and now she's upset. She told Butch she had to look for a new job because I was going to fire her; I'm thinking about it."

"I'll call her back."

"Good; don't tell her I told you anything because she'll die of humiliation."

Wren nodded. "I won't tell her."

Wren called Betsy. The phone rang so many times that Wren expected it to roll over to voice mail.

"Hello? What's wrong, Wren?" Betsy asked. "I almost didn't answer because...I was busy; that's it."

Ah, busy.

"I forgot to tell you something," Wren said.

"Really? About some guy? That's not it; there is no new guy, is there? It's the tornado: you and Rascal are badly hurt, aren't you? Are you in the hospital? Do you want me to tell Justin he has to come take care of you?"

"No, we weren't hurt in the tornado. I've been really homesick for Arizona. A man at the gas station told me that sunflowers like hot weather, so I bought a packet of sunflower seeds and have it in my truck next to my seat. I'll see my sunflower seeds wherever Rascal and I go; they'll remind me I can have sunflowers when I come back to Arizona."

"Really? Do you like this man at the gas station? What's his name? Maybe I'll get a seed packet of sunflowers too, so I'll remember you're coming back. I was afraid you would change your mind."

"Not likely; why would I do that?"

"Oh, I don't know; I'll bet there are a lot of cute guys in Texas." Betsy cleared her throat. "What if Justin changes his mind?"

"Then I'll still come back and beat him up."

Betsy laughed. "Good deal; maybe you should tell him that sometime because he's been mopey."

Wren rolled her eyes. *Who's mopey?*

"I guess I understand because I was in a funky mood the entire day until I bought my sunflower seeds."

"I must have sunflower seeds," Betsy mumbled. "I have to go; Justin and I have another meeting with one of the applicants this afternoon, then we meet with our lone male applicant tonight."

After they hung up, Wren said, "Maybe Justin isn't ignoring me; maybe he's swamped with work and the committee."

When Wren's phone rang, she stared at the display. *Why is that worm Blake calling me after dumping me four years ago? Why didn't I delete him from my contacts?*

Wren ignored the call. When her phone blinked the notification that she had a voice mail, she snorted. "I'll wait a couple of years then listen to it."

Her phone buzzed a text. Wren snorted again as she read it.

"Listen to this, Rascal: 'It's Blake; long time, no see, right?'" She deleted the text.

She opened her laptop and added a villain named Blake to the story. After she wrote three more pages, she reread her latest development with a wicked smile. "This is great; I might have to cut it later, but for now, it's therapy."

Her phone rang.

"Hi, Walt, where are you?"

"We finally made it to Aunt Jenna Lee's house. After the beauty shop, she decided she needed a pedicure. I'm still not clear why she couldn't have done that while she got her manicure, but there's no way I'm asking. I'm just grateful we're finally here. I asked Aunt Jenna Lee if I could look over the records in her safe, and she gave me this song and dance about she couldn't remember the combination, so I'm stuck."

"She told me Ralph Carson had the key to her safe."

"Really? I'm not totally surprised because Ralph's wife and Aunt Jenna Lee were close friends for a long time, in spite of the difference in their ages; I should have thought of it. I'll give him a quick call, thanks."

After he hung up, Wren wrinkled her nose. "I'm still in the middle of everybody's business, Rascal, but this time I think it was the right thing to do."

Rascal nosed the door; Wren went outside with him and relaxed in her yellow chair while Rascal wandered around the campsite.

When the work trucks entered the campground by way of the new entrance, Wren watched to see if Humberto had returned. "Not yet, Rascal, but this is the early crowd."

Her phone rang; she immediately answered.

"Howdy, stranger; how are you doing?" Wren asked.

Justin chuckled. "I deserved that; I officially hate the committee. Remind me to never be on a committee again. I'll call you later tonight, but I had to hear your voice. What's your day been like?"

"The day started off rough because I was in a mood; I went to the gas station, though, and bought new camping chairs, one is bright yellow, and the other one is green, and a packet of sunflower seeds, which has really lifted my spirits. When I was looking at the seed packets, one of the regular customers told me sunflowers love hot weather, so I instantly thought of Arizona. The picture of the bright, yellow sunflowers on the seed packet reminded me that it won't be long until I'll be back in Arizona. I'm keeping the packet in my truck, so every time Rascal and I go anywhere, I'll remember I'll soon be going to Arizona."

"You're amazing; I can feel all my stress melting. I'm really sorry, but I have to go. I miss you like crazy; I'll call you tonight."

"I miss you too."

After they hung up, tears slid down Wren's cheeks and splashed on her arm. She sniffled; Rascal followed her as she went inside.

Wren sat on the floor with Rascal, leaned against him, and sobbed. "I needed Justin to call me, and he did. I don't know why I'm crying; it was just so sweet and perfect."

When her tears slowed, Wren washed her face with cold water then peered into the mirror. "My eyes are red and puffy, but it was a good cry."

She sat at her dinette table. "It's time for that villain, Blake, to get what he deserves."

Wren typed in a frenzy to keep up with the story as it rapidly unfolded in her head. After an hour, she sat back. "Whoa, that was one furious ride."

She read over what she'd written. "I'll leave it for now; it's a little dark compared with the rest of the story, but I don't think Miranda would mind."

Her phone rang. *Walt.*

"Ralph brought his key to the safe then sat in the kitchen with Aunt Jenna Lee and drank coffee while I looked through as many of the folders and manila envelopes as I could. Have you had Aunt Jenna Lee's coffee? Ralph definitely took one for the team. The only documents in the safe that I saw in the forty minutes that I had were completed crossword pages that appeared to have been cut out of a booklet. I didn't find a will, power of attorney, or even the deed to this house. I'm positive she's squirreled away all those documents somewhere, but I don't know why or where. I talked to Ralph; he said he was afraid that all I'd find were old crossword puzzles because that's what Miss Jenna Lee put in the safe the last time he opened it for her."

"Normally, I'd say the direct approach is the best, but Miss Jenna Lee is a master at sidestepping questions she doesn't want to answer."

"Isn't that the truth; and to top it off, she doesn't know Ralph brought the key to the safe. I was supposedly napping while they talked. I'll call Ralph later; he might have some insights."

Wren sent Tara a text. "Nothing of interest in Miss JL's safe. Sorry."

Tara replied, "Drat. I had my hopes up. Talk to you tomorrow."

Wren stared out the window and smiled. "More trucks are returning; what do you think about sitting outside, Rascal? We can watch for Humberto."

Wren relaxed in her yellow chair and waved at the trucks; she grinned when she saw Humberto in the passenger's seat of one of the trucks. The truck stopped, and Humberto strode to her camper.

"You replaced your camping chairs; those bright colors are nice, Wren." He said on the green chair. "Comfortable too. So, I talked to the new guy who was telling people about a job. I asked him if he remembered what the man looked like, and he said the man was a local and described him as a big, old Texan with a moustache." Humberto chuckled. "Wren, he's a really young guy and not very tall, so to him, most of the men in the county would be big and old, and I'll bet eighty percent of the locals have a moustache."

"That is funny, but I guess I shouldn't be surprised; thanks for checking."

"It gets better. I asked him if he'd recognize the guy if he saw him, and he pointed at Dan and swore he was the man." Humberto snorted. "I've worked with Dan on other jobs; if Dan had a problem like that, half of the guys that work for him would have lined up to do whatever needed to be done, no questions asked, me included. He's one of the best, Wren."

"Definitely a dead end." Wren nodded.

Humberto's eyes twinkled as he rose from his chair. "The good news is that you, Tara, and Miss Jenna Lee are in the clear."

Wren giggled. "That's comforting, isn't it?"

Humberto chuckled as he strode to his camper while more trucks rolled in from the new entrance.

When Zuri suddenly roared in anger, Wren leapt out of her chair and scanned the campground in terror.

"Do you hear Zuri, Rascal? Something's terribly wrong."

Rascal's hackles rose. Wren glanced at the men who had parked and were climbing out of their trucks with no reactions that indicated anything was amiss.

Don't they hear Zuri?

As Zuri's roar of fury continued, Kendra parked in front of Wren's camper and smiled as she climbed out of her car.

"This looks pleasant; I love the bright colors of your chairs."

Wren spoke loudly, so she could be heard over the animal's howl. "You don't hear anything?"

Kendra tilted her head as she peered at Wren. "I hear the wind blowing in the treetops; are you still skittish from the tornado? That happens to a lot of people."

Zuri's loud cries became moans, then she was silent.

Wren narrowed her eyes. *I'm not jumpy. Something agitated Zuri, but I must be the only one who heard her.*

She exhaled. "You might be right; I've never seen this much damage from a tornado before. Are you on your way home?"

"Eventually; I need to go to the gas station and get a few things. Would you and Rascal like to ride along? I go past the campground on my way home, so I could drop you off."

"I'd enjoy it."

"Or better yet, I've been meaning to invite you to have supper with us; Gage is coming, so you could go home with me from the gas station, then he could give you a ride home at the end of the evening, and you could grill him about Tara."

Wren smiled. "That sounds like a perfect way to top off an evening. I'll pack Rascal's supper, so he can eat at his regular time."

After Wren and Rascal joined Kendra in her car, Kendra headed toward the gas station.

"Walt will sneak Rascal extra treats," Kendra said.

Wren grinned. "He thinks he's being sneaky, and so does Rascal; they have a conspiracy pact."

Kendra laughed. "Exactly; after he gets the campground at a point where it's not consuming him around the clock, I suspect we'll have a houseful of dogs and a field full of donkeys. In fact, I'll bet he'll want more than one cat in our barn as soon as we get one. Speaking of which, Walt called me right before I left. Ralph told him the vet said his mama dog was getting too old to breed, so Ralph was planning to surrender her to the vet or the county for rehoming."

"Really? I guess people do that sometimes with old dogs, but I don't understand it."

"I don't either; I'll bet you can tell me the rest of my story."

Rascal grinned, and Wren giggled. "Walt's bringing the old girl home with him, isn't he?"

"Sure is, and I'm tickled about it."

"So, what will you do while Walt works on his donkey rescue program?"

"I'm on the list for training through the county court system to support at-risk juveniles; we'll see where that goes."

"My grandma would say that y'all are full-plate people."

"I think we are; she must have been the same."

"Still is." Wren grinned. "Mom wants Grandma to slow down; Dad told me it's like watching a battle of the behemoths, and he has no intention of getting in the middle."

"I really appreciate that you told me about Aunt Jenna Lee and her crossword puzzles; it made me realize that she's doing everything she can to keep her mind active, and the campground is a big part of that, isn't it?"

Wren nodded. "She'd never admit it, but she enjoys the contact with people; she wouldn't do well at all if she wasn't involved with the service side of the campground."

Kendra chuckled. "Her version of customer service is definitely unique, isn't it?"

Wren smiled. "Jenna Lee style."

The gas station was busy when they arrived. Kendra slipped into the last parking spot at the far end of the store that was near the woods. Wren rolled her eyes when she recognized Nelson Decker's car. *I wonder if he's in there trying to avoid apologizing.*

"Are you coming in?" Kendra asked.

Rascal whined as he stared at the woods next to the store.

"I might in a few minutes," Wren said. "Rascal and I will take a short walk in the woods, so he can explore."

When they reached the edge of the woods, the man who helped her find the camping chairs strolled out of the gas station and joined them.

"You might want to go inside with Miss Kendra, Wren; there's nothing good out here."

Rascal darted into the woods.

"I will in a minute; I'd like to keep an eye on Rascal."

The man's face saddened, and he headed back to the store.

Chapter Thirteen

When Wren stepped in between the trees, the air temperature drastically dropped, and a sudden chill slid down her spine.

She peered around her and listened, but she couldn't see or hear Rascal. *There aren't any birds singing; maybe I am skittish.*

Her voice cracked as she whispered, "Rascal?"

Rascal whimpered. *I can barely hear him.*

"Rascal, come here, boy," Wren called out.

Rascal barked, and Wren hurried in the direction of his bark.

"Rascal?"

He joined her then whined and took a few steps farther into the woods then turned to look at her.

"Let's go back to the gas station, Rascal."

Rascal went a few feet farther into the woods and growled.

Wren swallowed hard then joined him and stared at the body on the ground that was covered with dead leaves. She grabbed onto a branch to keep from fainting. She picked up a stick and moved away the leaves from the man's head; Nelson Decker's dead eyes stared at her.

Wren screamed as she turned to run away; her feet were caught in a tangle vine, and she fell on her face. She scrambled to her feet and swallowed hard. "Let's go, Rascal."

When she neared the edge of the woods, she called nine-one-one.

"Whatcha got, Wren?" the dispatcher asked.

Wren's voice squeaked; she cleared her throat. "Nelson Decker is dead in the woods next to the gas station."

The man from the gas station stood next to her, and Wren relaxed.

"Sheriff and his deputy are on the way. Will you be okay?" the dispatcher asked.

Wren gazed at the man's kind face. "I'll be fine."

"Sirens," the man said.

Wren listened then heard them.

"They'll be here soon. Stay close to your good people; you know who they are." The man strolled away through the trees; Rascal leaned against Wren while she watched the man suddenly disappear in the shadows.

The deputy called out, "Wren!"

"We're here."

Rascal barked until the deputy reached them.

"You're shaking, Wren." The deputy put his arm around her and walked her out of the woods.

The sheriff met them at the edge. "Can Rascal show the deputy where the body is?"

Rascal barked, and the sheriff took Wren's elbow as the deputy reluctantly released her.

Rascal barked again then led the deputy into the woods.

"Let's sit in my cruiser; we're starting to draw a crowd." The sheriff opened the door to the passenger's seat then helped her in. After he closed the door, he strode to the driver's side and joined them.

"Go at your own pace, Wren," the sheriff said.

Wren nodded. "Rascal and I rode with Kendra to the gas station, so she could pick up a few things for supper; she invited us to eat at her house. I thought Rascal wanted a break, so I followed him to the grass, but he ran into the woods."

She turned to face the sheriff. "I followed Rascal and saw the body on the ground; it was almost completely covered by leaves. I took a stick and moved a few leaves away and recognized Nelson Decker."

Her smile was weak. "I screamed like a girl, then my feet got tangled in some vines, and I fell flat on my face."

The sheriff choked as he tried to stifle his chuckle. "Lord, you are something, Wren."

Wren exhaled. "Thank you, I think."

"I'll have Kendra pull her car close to my cruiser, then you can leave. I'll check in with you later; is that okay?"

Wren nodded in relief. "Yes, sir."

Rascal trotted to the cruiser as the sheriff returned from talking with Kendra. The sheriff opened the passenger's door for Wren.

"Wren, my deputy found a shallow hole and a shovel close to the body. We think you interrupted the killer, which is why the leaves were tossed over the body. I talked to Kendra; she would like for you to stay with them tonight, and I'd appreciate it. I'm calling your marshal in Arizona too."

Wren swallowed. "Okay."

The man's words echoed in her head as she climbed out of the cruiser. *Stay close to your good people; you know who they are.*

Wren frowned. *Why didn't I mention my friend to the sheriff?*

Wren and Rascal hopped into Kendra's car; as she turned onto the road, Kendra asked, "Are you okay, Wren?"

Wren blinked then side-glanced Kendra and giggled.

Kendra snorted. "It was bad, wasn't it? I have another equally obvious question, but maybe it isn't as klutzy. Would you like to stop by your camper to pick up your computer and a few things for our sleepover party?"

"Sounds perfect; I'd like to tell Humberto that I'm okay too because you know word will get around fast."

"You're right; I thought we'd go into the office early before Aunt Jenna Lee comes in to take care of any overnight reservations. What do you think?"

"I think it's a good idea to check, but don't do anything, so Miss Jenna Lee will have something to do; otherwise, she'll think you're trying to shove her aside."

"I didn't think of that; thanks for keeping me out of trouble. Harper told me we just missed Walt. He stopped by and bought a new collar, two different dog beds, senior dog food, treats, water and food bowls, and a few toys. I don't even know what our dog's name is. Did Ralph ever mention her to you?"

"He said the mama of the puppies was a Labrador retriever, but he didn't mention her name."

Kendra glanced in her rearview mirror. "Rascal's relaxed; that's very comforting."

After Kendra parked in front of Wren's camper, she stayed outside with Rascal while Wren went inside and packed overnight clothes and toiletries and her laptop. On a whim, she added Miranda's stories to her computer bag then carried out her computer bag and her tote bag with her clothes and other items.

Wren smiled as she put her bags in the back on the floorboard. "I'm all packed and ready for my first sleepover."

"I don't think I've ever gone to a sleepover either, except when we visited relatives, and that absolutely doesn't count because my cousins were little brats."

Wren glanced toward Humberto's camper; he stepped outside then strode toward her.

"You've heard?" Wren asked when he joined her in front of her camper.

"Just now; I'm really scared for you, Wren; I haven't heard from Tara, so you might want to call her right away." Humberto glanced at Kendra. He lowered his voice. "Are you going to stay with the Navarros? That's excellent; you know where I am if you need me, and you have my cell number. Text or call anytime, but I already told you that." Humberto smiled. "See you later."

On the way to her house, Kendra said, "Tell me about your guy, or tell me it's none of my business; I'm okay either way."

"His name is Justin; he's a county marshal in Arizona, and we're just starting to become acquainted."

"Whoa, start at the beginning because this sounds like it's going to be a fascinating story."

Wren giggled. "There's not much to tell, really. He's kind-hearted and funny."

"Your story definitely has potential, doesn't it? What are the next steps?"

"My assignment is to write articles about four haunted campgrounds; Arizona was my first and this is my second."

"Do you know where you're going next?"

"Not yet; I'm waiting to hear that my article for the Lonesome Trail Campground is accepted, then Charlie, he's the publisher, will tell me where my next assignment is. There is one other twist. I'm assessing different camping trailers for the manufacturer who is interested in marketing to young, single campers, so I have a new camper every assignment."

"That is really interesting, so four different campgrounds with four different trailers? Have you always been interested in camping?"

Wren smiled. "I grew up camping, but I didn't realize how sheltered I was from the hard work of hooking up to a trailer and the operations of the water, sewer, and the water heater. I expected to learn how to light an oven, but neither one of my campers had one, which was a huge shock to me; Mom always warmed up cinnamon rolls for breakfast after we got our trailer." Wren rolled her eyes. "My world of camping was to jump in a car or truck, go camping, have a great time, then go home."

Kendra laughed. "Ah, the innocence of youth. Tell me about Rascal."

"Rascal is a black and tan Labrador Retriever with Husky mixed in somewhere along the way, according to our vet. Dad and I found him at our local county animal shelter when he was not quite two years old; he's four now. The shelter told us we were his fifth owners; he had a knack for escaping and running away. Our vet told Dad Rascal must have been looking for me because he's always been by my side. He has an odd twist to one leg, and he runs a little funny because of it. Our vet thinks he was probably hit by a car when he was a young pup, and it wasn't treated properly. He'll probably have arthritis when he gets older, but there are good medications now, so old dogs don't have to suffer with the pain these days. I've always been a freelance writer, so we're rarely apart."

"Back to Justin: what are the next steps?" Kendra asked.

"After I finish my fourth article, I'm going back to Arizona."

"What if things don't work out with Justin?"

"Then I'll never wonder what might have been."

"Would you stay in Arizona?"

"No telling; if we don't part friendly, I might just stay to torment him."

Kendra snort-laughed. After she wiped her eyes, she said, "I love your style."

Kendra pulled into a long driveway; when she parked in front of an old farm style house with white clapboard siding and an oversized, covered porch, she said, "Let me see a picture of Justin, then let's go meet my husband's new girlfriend."

Rascal whined. "And Rascal's new girlfriend too," Kendra added.

Wren pulled up Justin's selfie and showed Kendra.

"Wow, he's a really good-looking guy, and he's obviously totally smitten with you from the look in his eye and that cute grin."

Wren giggled. "I hope so."

When they went into the house, an old chocolate lab with a gray muzzle grinned as she joyfully wagged her tail. When Rascal approached her, she raised her head in a regal pose, and Wren squealed. "You are so pretty. What's her name?"

"I called her Ruby, and she seemed to like it," Walt said.

"Is that it, Ruby? Is that your name?" Kendra asked.

Ruby grinned, and Kendra laughed. "Smart girl, Ruby."

While Walt took the groceries from Kendra, she said, "Wren's going to spend the weekend with us."

Walt nodded. "I heard; does anyone know you'll be here?"

"Humberto guessed," Wren said.

"That's fine; he won't say anything. Wren, the sheriff called me, so I don't have the gossip version."

He knows about the shovel but doesn't want to mention it in front of Kendra.

"I'll show you your bedroom, Wren, then if you want to set up your computer in the kitchen to keep me company while I cook, I promise I'll interrupt you only when it's critical," Kendra said.

Walt laughed; when Kendra glared at him, he chuckled as he invited Ruby and Rascal to go outside to walk with him and explore.

While Wren set up her laptop, Kendra said, "I feel like oven fried chicken and potato salad; what do you think?"

"Sounds good to me."

Kendra scrubbed potatoes then cut them into cubes and dropped them into a pot. "You mentioned that you're waiting to hear whether your article is accepted. Does that mean a few edits to update if it isn't accepted?"

Wren smiled. "My publisher and I were tangled in a war over his editor who dictated a complete rewrite with a main character and plot of the editor's choosing in my first article. It came to a showdown: accept the article as is, or take over my job because I'll quit. Either the editor changed his mind, or the publisher managed to assuage the editor's irrational insistence on his main character. The last email I received from my publisher was that the editor insisted I rewrite the Lonesome Trail article to match the first, which was a completely irrational response. Both articles respect the local legends. I believe that is important for the series of articles."

"Remind me: what type of magazine is this?"

"It's a travel magazine."

"That idiot editor needs to find a job at a true crimes magazine if he wants to write a police blotter," Kendra growled.

Wren checked her email and exhaled.

"That was a long sigh; what was that for?" Kendra asked.

"I have an email from my publisher."

"Read it to me; oops, that sounded bossy. How's this? Read it to me or else, girly." Kendra spoke out of the side of her mouth like a 1930's gangster.

"Much smoother," Wren laughed.

Wren read the email. "This is so Charlie, listen to this. 'The editor is traveling and is not available this weekend; please be ready to leave Monday morning after we complete our review. As ever, Charlie.'"

"I have so many inappropriate words for Charlie and his editor," Kendra said.

While Kendra put the eggs on the stove to steam as part of her preparation in making potato salad, Wren's phone rang.

When she answered, Betsy asked, "Are you busy? Never mind, I don't care. You have to talk to me."

"Okay, go ahead," Wren said.

Wren glanced at Kendra, who raised her eyebrows.

"A friend from Arizona," Wren said.

"Of course, I'm a friend from Arizona; that's exactly why I'm calling you. You won't believe who just left the office; go ahead, guess. You'll never guess. Actually, I don't really know who it was, so you could guess anyone, and you could be right." Betsy took a breath.

"Can you slow down just a little bit?" Wren asked.

Betsy exhaled.

"A nice-looking young man came into the office; he was very polite; I knew right away that he wasn't from around here because he kind of talked like you. He said he was from the travel magazine and gave me a business card. The name on the card was Charlie Hogue."

"Charlie? He's not young at all."

"I didn't think so from what you've said, so when he told me he was there to verify your article and asked me if I knew you, I said no. He told me I must know you because you stayed here last week. I told him that I don't have time to socialize with our guests."

"I wonder if he was Charlie's editor; Charlie told me the editor was traveling; he said he was there to verify my article? What a jerk."

"I didn't think of that; he became very agitated and told me he'd come a long way to make sure your article was accurate, and I told him to get out. I picked up my phone and took a quick photo of the man while he raved on then texted Butch our code word that means I'm in trouble. When Butch barreled into the office, the young man had raised his voice and claimed I was lying."

"Did Butch scare him?"

Betsy giggled. "He sure did; he roared for the man to get out or he'd have him arrested for assault. The man said he wasn't assaulting anybody, and Butch put his fist in front of the man's face and practically growled, 'You're about to assault my knuckles.'"

Wren laughed. "No, he really said that?"

"I almost fainted; I've never heard him talk like that before. The man was in such a hurry to get out that he tripped over the doorjamb and twisted his ankle. After he hobbled to his car and fled, I told Butch what I just told you, and he said I should call you. Should I call Justin?"

"You took a picture of him; could you text it to me?"

"Sure; that's a great idea." Betsy hung up.

Wren stared at her phone then sighed.

"What's wrong?" Kendra asked.

"A man showed up at the Forgotten Oasis Campground and told Betsy he was there to verify the facts of my article; he gave her my publisher's business card. I got a little lost in her convoluted story about how obnoxious he was, but Betsy took a picture of him before her husband chased off the man; she's texting the photo to me."

"She was upset but still managed to have the presence of mind to snap a photo? I think Betsy's amazing."

Wren's phone rang; when she answered it, Betsy asked, "Did you get it?"

"No, not yet."

"Okay, let me try again." Betsy hung up.

"Betsy's having technical difficulties," Wren said.

Wren stared at her silent phone until Kendra gently put her hand on Wren's shoulder. "How about a glass of sweet tea?"

Wren nodded.

Kendra poured two glasses of tea then joined Wren at the table.

After Wren's phone buzzed a text, she immediately replied, "Got it."

Wren looked at the photo and snarled, "It's Blake! What a weasel!"

Kendra's eyes widened. "Who's Blake?"

"No good, two-timer," Wren growled. "I can't believe it. I'm going to call Charlie right now and blast his eardrums."

"Whoa, slow down, Wren; take a breath and tell me what's going on."

Wren inhaled then exhaled slowly as she shook her head. "This is unbelievable." She snorted. "If I was going to write this in a story, we'd be sitting in a smoke-filled bar, tossing down shots of whiskey. No, maybe we'd be…"

Kendra narrowed her eyes. "Wren, if you don't tell me right now, I'm taking away your glass of tea and cutting you off the rest of the night."

Wren side-glanced Kendra and clutched her glass with both hands. "Blake and I met in a journalism class our freshman year and were practically inseparable. By our junior year, we had made serious plans for a future together after we graduated."

"I think I'm not going to like Blake," Kendra said.

Wren bit her lip. "The last half of our senior year Blake met Briar Monroe in the coffee shop that was close to campus, and she was all he talked about from that day on. Blake told me Briar's parents named her Briana, but she had decided the previous year that Briar was edgier. I'd never really met her, but I knew who she was; she was part of the popular clique: everyone knew Briar. She was tall, athletic, blond, and a polished extrovert, which is everything that I was not. Blake told me she was super smart because she was a political science major and that her parents had connections in the publishing industry; when he told me she would make sure he got a great job in New York City while she went to law school there, I was crushed, and he didn't even notice. They were engaged before we graduated. I heard she dumped him the day before the wedding for the son of a lawyer who had connections at the law school in New York City."

"Couldn't have happened to a nicer guy," Kendra said.

Wren nodded then downed her glass of sweet tea. She set down her glass hard on the table. "Another round here, barkeep."

Kendra laughed then growled in a low-pitched drawl. "Y'all better take it easy, there, chickie."

Wren smiled. "It stung for a long time. Looking back, Blake was very critical of my writing style in our journalism class; I took the easy route and switched my major to English literature while he stayed in journalism."

"That's so ironic because you became a successful journalist while he's a no-talent leech trying to hijack other people's hard work."

After Kendra refilled both their glasses, Wren pointed to her phone on the table, and Kendra picked it up and examined the photo.

Wren continued, "He has the same dark-brown hair, except with a more stylish cut; he was never stylish in college. He's still wearing glasses, which doesn't surprise me because he tried, without success, for three weeks the first part of our sophomore year to insert his new contact lenses. That look on his face..." Wren sighed. "It's so funny how well I knew him, then suddenly, I didn't know him at all."

"Did he try to reconnect with you after Briar dumped him?"

Wren chuckled. "Only one time; I told him I couldn't talk very long because Briar and I were meeting for lunch in fifteen minutes to discuss a job opportunity she had for me."

Kendra laughed. "I love it."

"I knew that Blake had an uncle who was a publisher, but I never dreamed it was Charlie."

"What are you going to tell Betsy?"

"I'll call Charlie first; I think I'll play ignorant on this one."

"Is it okay if I listen while I wash and dice celery and peel the steamed eggs?"

"It's fine." Wren tapped in Charlie's number.

When Charlie answered, Wren said, "Charlie, the campground manager in Arizona called me earlier; there was a man asking about me and what I was doing. She called the local marshal, and he contacted the Arizona state police. I'm sure they'll get in touch with you, so I wanted you to know that I'm safe. The marshal called the sheriff here to give him a heads-up because he is certain that someone is stalking me."

"What? A marshal in Arizona and the sheriff in Texas? But..."

"I know you're worried because I'm haven't been in Texas very long, but the sheriff is good friends with the campground owners and is in contact with the Texas Rangers. Everyone is on high alert for anyone asking about me."

"Wren, you..."

She interrupted. "I know; we'll just have to see when the Texas Rangers think it's safe for me to travel. Do you already have my next assignment lined up?"

"No, well, actually, I might."

"Let me know as soon as it's firm, and I'll talk to the sheriff, so he can intercede for me with the Texas Rangers."

Charlie cleared his throat. "I have a few things to do, then I'll get back to you."

Wren hung up; her eyes twinkled as she asked, "What do you think? How did I do?"

"I think I have to sit on the front porch all night with my shotgun in case that dastardly stalker decides to do any skulking around here."

Kendra narrowed her eyes as she slowly scanned the kitchen. "If that smelly outlaw dares to show his face at my dining table, he ain't helpin' hisself to no dessert."

Wren laughed. "If I ever decide to write an Old West novel, will you help me with the dialog?"

Kendra grinned. "Sure 'nuff, ma'am; happy to oblige."

Walt, Rascal, and Ruby came into the house.

Walt kissed Kendra on the cheek and smiled. "We heard laughing, so we thought it might be safe to come inside. Rascal and Ruby are ready for their supper. Do you have Rascal's food, Wren?"

"Sure, do you know if Ruby is food-aggressive?"

"No, but Rascal would know. If I show you where I intend to feed Ruby, I think Rascal can decide where he wants to eat."

After Walt and Wren dished up the food for their respective dogs, Walt stood near the utility room.

Rascal yipped then trotted to the other side of the kitchen. While the two dogs ate, Walt shook his head. "I wouldn't have thought she would be food-aggressive."

Wren furrowed her brow. "I don't think she is. I think Rascal is giving her space to enjoy her food because she probably has had very little of it in her life."

Kendra put her hand over her heart. "We'll make sure she has all the space she wants."

"What do you think about onion in potato salad, Wren?" Kendra asked.

"I'm okay either..."

Walt turned his back to Kendra and held up a thumb where only Wren could see.

Wren continued, "...way, but I actually prefer onion."

"Alrighty then; onion it is." Kendra peeled an onion then finely diced half of it.

Chapter Fourteen

Walt poured himself a glass of sweet tea. "Ruby enjoyed the romp with Rascal. He let her set the pace; he's really a special guy, Wren."

"Yes, he is." Wren rubbed his face then hugged him.

"When do we expect Gage?" Walt asked.

"Haven't heard anything, so I expect when he walks in the door," Kendra said.

Wren's phone buzzed a text from Tara. "Gage is a pest. Mama's a softie; she's feeding him."

Wren giggled. "According to the text I just got from Tara, we shouldn't expect Gage for dinner this evening."

Wren read the text aloud.

"Tell Tara thanks for me," Kendra said.

"Nope, don't do it," Walt said. "We don't need to get Gage in trouble with Tara."

"What makes you the expert on what makes young women angry?" Kendra asked.

"In case you haven't noticed, I'm married to one," Walt said.

Kendra giggled. "Dang, you are so good sometimes."

When Walt left the kitchen to relax in front of the television, Ruby padded along with him; Rascal stayed in the kitchen with Wren.

Wren opened her laptop and smiled. *I know what happens next in the story.*

She smiled as she typed as quickly as she could; when she looked up, she and Rascal were alone in the kitchen. She inhaled the heady aroma of herbed chicken in the oven.

"The kitchen smells good; I got lost in my story, didn't I?" Wren smiled as she stretched. "Where is everyone?"

Rascal nosed the back door; when they went outside, Kendra and Walt were holding hands; Ruby grinned.

"Sorry," Wren said, "I fell into my story."

"I can't wait to read it," Kendra said.

"I'll hear all the good parts while Kendra reads it." Walt winked, and Wren giggled.

"The chicken's probably ready to come out of the oven." Kendra rose from her chair.

While everyone went inside, Wren's phone buzzed.

She smiled at Justin's text: "Betsy called me; are you safe with good people?"

Wren responded, "Yes."

"Good. Will call later. Betsy said come back to Arizona. Or maybe I did."

Wren's eyes welled up as she responded. "Thank you."

"Was it Justin?" Kendra asked.

"Yes."

"Is that bad? Do I know who Justin is?" Walt glanced at Wren while he pulled out the potato salad from the refrigerator.

Kendra removed the chicken from the oven. "It's not bad; Justin is the marshal in Arizona, and we like him," Kendra said.

"We do? You too?" Walt peered at Wren.

"Yes, me too."

"Okay, so..." Walt glanced at Kendra who glowered at him.

Walt continued, "...are we ready to eat?"

After they ate, Walt asked, "Is there something going on in Arizona that I need to worry about?"

"Not really," Wren said. "I'm mad at my publisher because I just found out his jerk of an editor is probably an ex-friend of mine."

"A scum of an old boyfriend," Kendra added.

"Let me know if you need any help; I've always wanted to be the enraged dad," Walt said.

"He showed up at the campground in Arizona; he implied he was the publisher and claimed he was there to verify the article I wrote about the campground. The campground manager's husband chased him off," Wren said.

After Kendra and Wren put away the leftovers, and Walt turned on the dishwasher, Wren and Walt went outside with Rascal and Ruby.

While Wren and Walt relaxed on the back porch, Rascal chased grasshoppers, and Ruby investigated the yard then flopped down on the grass. "I'm taking her to the vet on Monday for a good checkup then to a groomer for a bath and some pampering," Walt said. "Ralph said she had a checkup before her last batch of puppies, but I'd like to get her established with a vet closer to us."

"I think she'll love the pampering," Wren said.

After Ruby rolled in the grass, she joined Rascal in chasing grasshoppers.

Walt chuckled. "I think Rascal is showing her how to play. The exercise will be good for her."

Walt rose from his chair. "My favorite show comes on in five minutes. Come on, Ruby; let's go inside."

Wren smiled as Ruby trotted to Walt while Rascal continued to jump for grasshoppers.

Wren gazed at the changing colors in the sky as the sun slowly set and sighed. "I forgot about Blake's voice mail, Rascal. I should probably listen to it."

She picked up her phone, but before she checked her voice mail, her phone rang.

Wren answered Charlie's call.

"I wanted you to know that I've sent your article to the printer; your idea of keeping your articles true to the legends will appeal to our readers and have them eager to read the next article. I have your next assignment ready. You can pick up your new camper in Waco."

"Thank you. I'll have to talk to the sheriff first to ask when the Texas Rangers will allow me to leave."

"I forgot about that. Give the sheriff a call then call me right back, so I can give you the coordinates of the campground in Tennessee. It will take you three days to get there, so if you leave in the morning, you'll be there Monday afternoon."

"I'll call you tomorrow with an estimate of when I can leave; I'll need to allow extra time to pick up the new camper, but we can talk about that tomorrow. Nice talking to you, Charlie; have a great evening."

Wren hung up; when she smacked a second mosquito, she listened to Blake's voice mail.

"Hey, there, Wrennie. So, I thought I'd drop in to see how you're doing. That campground must be a dump; I can't believe how far it is from Phoenix. See ya soon!"

Wren disconnected from her voicemail. "What a jerk; he never called me Wrennie. Let's go inside, Rascal."

Kendra looked up from her book when Wren joined her at the kitchen table. "Did you get a phone call from Justin?"

"Not yet; Charlie called to tell me he sent my article to the printer."

"That's good, right?" Kendra asked.

"It really is. I'll talk to the sheriff about when he thinks it will be safe for me to leave here."

"Leave? You don't get a little break?"

"Not according to Charlie, but I'm taking one."

"I just remembered we talked about making cowboy cookies. Are you too tired?"

"Not at all; I'd enjoy it."

Kendra pulled out her recipe notebook. "I got the recipe from Walt's abuela. Walt's mother helped me translate it from Spanish then I typed it. Walt swears they taste exactly like his grandmother's, but I think he just wants to be sure I keep making them."

Kendra pulled out the ingredients and handed them to Wren, who placed them on the kitchen table. Kendra put her stand mixer on the counter, and they measured and mixed the ingredients.

After the first tray went into the oven, Wren dropped generous portions of cookie dough on a second tray while Kendra unloaded then reloaded the dishwasher.

Kendra put in the third tray of cookies while the first one was cooling. "This is going much faster than when I do this alone; thanks for the help, Wren. Put four cookies on a plate and take it to Walt, would you?"

"Won't that make me a celebrity?" Wren asked.

"Probably, but you need the boost." Kendra grinned. "Wait, one more thing." Kendra poured a glass of milk. "He'll probably have to come back for more cookies to meet his required cookie to milk ratio, but this is a good start."

When Wren took the plate and glass into the family room, Walt grinned as he muted the television. "I smelled cookies in the oven, and I was hoping they'd be cowboy cookies. These are larger than usual; I'll bet you made them, didn't you?"

Wren beamed.

Walt bit into a cookie and closed his eyes. "Absolute perfection; better than Abuela ever made."

Wren returned to the kitchen. "Walt is definitely a cowboy cookie fan, and you're right that it was a boost for me; I felt like a cookie rock star. Would it be okay if I snap a photo of the recipe? I think Justin would love them as much as Walt does."

Kendra opened her binder to the cowboy cookie recipe. "Go right ahead, but you'll have to let me know what Justin thinks. If he hates them, then dump him and come back here to live with us; we'll talk trash about that man who doesn't have sense enough to love cowboy cookies."

Wren giggled. "It's always good to have a backup plan."

Kendra smiled as Wren tried to cover her yawn.

"It's getting late, but I want to wait up for Justin to call me. I'm tired of my T-shirt, socks, and jeans; if it's okay with you, I'll go to my room and put on my comfy clothes."

"I understand that completely; I have what I call my lounging outfit: a comfortable, oversized, faded red Texas Tech T-shirt that Walt gave me when I was pregnant with Gage and a pair of red and black plaid flannel pajama pants I bought when Walt announced we were going skiing twenty-five years ago."

"I've never been skiing; did you enjoy it?"

"I had four full days' worth of lessons but wasn't allowed on the bunny slope because I just couldn't get the hang of it. I am proud that I completely mastered falling down without getting hurt, and I absolutely loved it. Don't worry about trying to get up early; Walt will walk Ruby and Rascal and feed them in the morning while I cook his breakfast. I'll have breakfast with you."

"I usually wake up before the sun rises."

"If you wake, and no one else is up, push the button on the coffee maker if it hasn't already started. I have it set to be ready by six. If you'd like to shower tonight or in the morning, the bathroom next to your bedroom has towels, soap, and shampoo for guests, which so far have been Mama and you. Gage has a room here too, but since he moved into his house, he doesn't use his room at all. I may repurpose it for something; I don't quite know what."

"I may shower tonight and tomorrow morning just for the luxury of taking a non-claustrophobic shower. I've been taking showers in the tiny camper shower; I can put my hands on my hips and touch the sides of the shower with my elbows."

"Wow, and you're petite. Why do they do that?"

"It's probably meant to be only for occasional use, but I'm not crazy about the whole process of collecting all my shower things and hauling them across the campground to the shower, especially since half the time I forget something. The worst part is that I always seem to get my dry clothes wet from the shower floor when I try to get dressed."

Wren glanced at Kendra. "This is not only boring, it's a little whiny, isn't it?"

Kendra smiled. "Let's call it normal, which we haven't had much of today. It was interesting to hear about a decision our guests face regularly at our campground that I knew nothing about."

"Thank you." Wren sighed.

"Go take your shower; I think you'll feel a lot better."

Wren picked up her computer and went into her new bedroom then checked the time. *I have time for a shower before Justin calls if I hurry.*

She carried her phone, comfortable clothes, and toiletries to the bathroom; after she brushed her teeth, she climbed into the shower and sighed as the hot water sprayed over her and soothed her tense muscles.

Hot water, lots of room. Wren smiled as she shampooed her hair. *Cowboy cookies are Walt's favorite treat; a hot shower is my version of cowboy cookies.*

After Wren dried and put on her mint-green sweatpants with her soft, vanilla cream T-shirt of a smiling sloth hanging upside down on a branch in the middle of the T-shirt, she and Rascal, who had been waiting for her in the hall, went to her bedroom.

While Wren fluffed the pillows then sat on the bed with her computer, Rascal blocked the closed door when he flopped down then closed his eyes.

Wren wrote what she'd been planning to have happen next in her novel then rested with her hands still on the keyboard.

Her ringing phone woke her. She glanced at her computer screen then snorted at the continuous lines of the letter 'e' she had typed when she had fallen asleep.

When she answered, Justin asked, "Is it too late for me to call?"

"Not at all; I've been writing."

"Are you working on your novel? How's it going?"

"I thought I would be farther along than I am. I've never written fiction before; I think I misjudged how long writing a novel takes. How are you doing?"

"This committee stuff has really been interfering with work. I talked to the school superintendent and the chairperson of the school board today and told them that unless the school board had any additional candidates for us to screen, there was no reason for the screening committee to continue meeting. I think they were trying to push the decision of who to hire onto the screening committee."

"What did they say?"

"They moaned and groaned but didn't have an argument, so they finally agreed. What about your day other than finding another dead man?" Justin asked.

"The sheriff told me he was going to call you; I'm glad he did. I heard back from Charlie; he sent my article about the campground here to the printer and has the electronic version scheduled for distribution. I'll be going to Tennessee, but I don't know where yet. He wanted me to leave in the morning, but I told him I'd have to talk to the sheriff about when it's okay for me to leave."

"How could he expect you to leave in the morning if you didn't know where you were going?"

"I kind of cut him off; leaving in the morning was a completely unreasonable expectation on his part. He told me it would take me three days to get to the campground, but he didn't allow any time for picking up the new camper in Waco, much less any time for an adequate walk-through."

"Head this way, anytime," Justin said. "Or stay where you are, and I'll come get you; I could probably fly into Waco."

Tears welled up in her eyes; Wren smiled. "I'm so grateful that you're my backup. Thank you."

Justin sighed. "You're halfway finished with your assignment; I know you won't quit."

Wren giggled. "Charlie doesn't know that; I guess he's really counting on the haunted campground series to help boost the magazine, or else the RV manufacturer's advertising money is his motivation, but he's been relatively cooperative so far when I mention that I can walk away from the assignment."

Justin chuckled. "What else is going on?"

"I learned how to make cowboy cookies; I have the recipe, and I'll make a batch when I come to Arizona."

Wren furrowed her brow. "There is one other thing; I don't think anyone except you would understand. Remember the gaiters I bought at the gas station? One of the customers, an older man, helped me find them and pick out the size. He told me to keep Rascal close to me because not everyone is what they seem."

"That was the first time you met him?" Justin asked.

"Yes, then another time at the gas station, I heard two women gossiping in a very mean way about Walt, the campground owner. The older man stood next to me and told me to ignore them because that's how they were, and I felt a lot better."

"He definitely has your best interests at heart; he sounds like a kind man."

"I do feel much better after he talks to me. When I was looking for new camping chairs, I was having a bad day because I was homesick for Arizona, and the older man told me that sunflowers grew in hot climates; I knew he was talking about Arizona. He understood I was feeling down and how to cheer me up."

When Wren grew quiet, Justin waited a few minutes before he said, "There's more; I'm listening."

"After I found the body in the woods next to the gas station, the older man stood with me while I called nine-one-one and stayed until the deputy and sheriff arrived. He told me to stay close to good people and added that I knew who they were."

"He's like Thomas, isn't he?" Justin asked.

"I think that's why I haven't mentioned him to anyone else."

"I agree with him about staying close to good people," Justin said. "Do you think the killer is someone you might know?"

"I don't know that many people, so I really don't."

"Your older man might know; seems like it's smart to listen to him. It's late there; sleep well and be safe."

After they hung up, Wren shut down her computer, turned off the light, and snuggled under the covers while she thought about Justin's crooked smile and snuggling with Justin.

Chapter Fifteen

Wren woke to a scratching noise at her bedroom door, and Rascal whined.

"Shh," Walt whispered, "we don't want to wake up Wren."

Wren made her way in the dark to the bedroom door; when she opened it, Rascal dashed out, and Ruby yipped.

"Sorry, Wren," Walt said. "If you can, you can go back to sleep, or there's coffee in the kitchen if you can't."

"Coffee," Wren said.

"Good choice. The dogs and I are going outside, then I'll feed them."

Wren padded barefoot to the kitchen and poured herself a cup of coffee then dropped an ice cube in it to cool it off.

While she sipped her coffee, she gazed at Justin's picture. *We should have thought of this earlier.*

Kendra joined her in the kitchen; after Kendra poured a cup, she joined Wren at the kitchen table. When Walt, Rascal, and Ruby came inside, Walt stopped to kiss Kendra before he fed the dogs.

"Do you have any preference for breakfast?" Kendra asked.

"How about eggs and grits?" Walt asked.

Kendra rose to go to the pantry. "Do you like grits, Wren?"

"I love grits."

"It's a huge bonus to have a southern girl who has been to Arizona here," Walt said. "She eats southern food and spicy, hot food."

Wren hurried to her bedroom and changed from her sweatpants and sloth T-shirt to jeans and a solid green T-shirt; after she stuck her holster on the inside of her waistband then slipped in her pistol, she patted her pistol then frowned at her shirt. *I need a yellow T-shirt. Maybe we'll go to the gas station later.*

While she made her bed, her phone buzzed a text from Justin. "Call when you can."

She immediately called. "Are you okay?"

"I had a nightmare and couldn't sleep. Are you still carrying your pistol?"

"Yes, is that what your nightmare was about?"

"I couldn't shake off the feeling that you will need your pistol today; I had to hear you say you had it."

"What was the nightmare about?"

Justin exhaled. "I don't remember much of it, but something drew Rascal away from you; you were ambushed and didn't have your pistol. That's when I woke in a sweat. I'm probably just nervous because you've found two bodies this week. I've been sort of worried that you won't want to come back, but now I'm worried that the killer might think you're stalking him."

"Honey, you know I'm coming back to Arizona, and I just finished dressing; getting dressed always includes my carry pistol."

Justin chuckled. "You called me honey; I'm okay now. I'll call you later."

After they hung up, Wren furrowed her brow. *What could draw Rascal away from me?*

She hurried to the kitchen as Kendra put a plate in front of Walt, who was sitting at the table.

"Sorry, I took longer than I expected."

"Your timing is perfect." Kendra set their plates on the table.

As Wren sat, she peered at the small bowl that was on her plate.

"I always put the grits in a small bowl because Gage didn't like his food touching when he was four; he grew out of it by the time he reached high school, but it had already become a habit for me."

Wren smiled. *I have a habit of patting my pistol after I put it into its holster. I never wondered why.*

While they ate breakfast, Walt asked, "What's the plan for today?"

"We're going to the office until Aunt Jenna Lee comes in, then I have an online training lesson to finish while Wren writes; we may come back here to focus," Kendra said. "If you don't take Ruby with you, she can spend the day with us."

"That might be a good idea. What do you think, Ruby?"

Ruby grinned.

After Walt left, Kendra cleaned the kitchen while Wren gathered her things.

On the way to the campground, Wren said, "When you talked about putting grits in a bowl because it became a habit, I thought it was really interesting that you knew exactly how it became a habit."

Kendra smiled. "It's totally obvious to me, but I don't think Walt or Gage could tell you why I put grits in a small bowl."

"Obvious," Wren repeated.

She furrowed her brow as her thoughts wandered. "Do you suppose that's where Miss Jenna Lee's will and deed are?"

"Somewhere obvious?" Kendra chuckled. "That's a little tricky if we're talking about something obvious to Aunt Jenna Lee."

Wren nodded. "The obvious place would have been her safe." *What was it my friend at the gas station said?* She gazed at the passing trees and fields. *Sometimes the obvious place to look isn't obvious at all.*

"Wherever they are must be obvious to her," Kendra said.

When they reached the campground, Ruby was hesitant to get out of the car. "What's wrong, Ruby?" Kendra asked. "You can stay with me in the office or go outside with Rascal."

Rascal yipped, and Ruby slowly climbed out of the car then followed Kendra into the office with Rascal at her side.

Kendra glanced around the office. "There are so many things I'd like to do to this office to give it the Lonesome Trail Railroad look while we wait for the new office building. Would I be stepping on Aunt Jenna Lee's toes?"

"Probably, but don't you think she'll complain about it for a week then suddenly announce it was her idea all along?"

Kendra smiled. "That's exactly what she would do. I'll sketch out my design plan first. I want it to be comfortable and inviting but not touristy, which sounds easy in my head just like every other time I've tackled a new design."

Wren's phone rang. *It's a little early for Betsy.*

"What are you doing up so early?"

"I have to ask you something, and it's very important, but I have to be quiet, so I don't wake up Butch."

"I'm listening."

"I got a phone call at the office from a woman named Nadine who said she lived in Dry Creek, Texas; she said she knew you, and you are a very attractive young woman, but she is worried about you."

"Can I tell you what someone told me about Nadine?"

"I guess so."

"He said if Nadine announced it was bright and sunny with no clouds in the sky, all the locals would run grab umbrellas."

"So, does that mean that anything she says doesn't have a grain of truth?"

"Pretty much; what did she say?"

"She said you were leading on a nice, local man named Gage and a young, naïve deputy, and she was concerned that you might be a little too flirty for a small town. She wanted to know how many hearts you've broken."

"What did you tell her?"

"I told her dozens; are you mad at me?"

Wren snort-laughed. "That was the perfect answer. Did you say anything to Justin?"

"See, that's the thing: I told him exactly what I told you. He asked me if you'd mentioned Gage or the deputy to me. Do you know either of them very well?"

I wonder if this has anything to do with Justin's worries and his nightmare. Wren frowned. *Why didn't he tell me what Betsy said or ask me about Gage or the deputy? Doesn't he trust me?*

"Gage and his dad own the campground, and the deputy is a nice guy. Gage is a good friend, but I don't know the deputy very well."

"I should have known she was trying to make trouble. I have to get off the phone because Butch will be a bear all day if I wake him up."

"Thanks for letting me know about Nadine. I'll talk to you later."

"What do I say if Nadine calls again?"

"Tell her you checked on me with an old friend of yours in Dry Creek and heard that Penny is talking about Nadine behind her back."

Betsy giggled. "You know I'd never do that, but if she calls, I'll laugh."

After Wren hung up, Rascal yipped, then he and Ruby trotted to the door.

"I guess we're going to tour the campground, Kendra. We won't be long," Wren said.

Rascal trotted ahead of Wren with Ruby by his side.

"Let's stop at our camper a minute, Rascal; I have to send a text to the sheriff."

While Rascal and Ruby relaxed in the shade, Wren went inside the camper and texted the sheriff. "Call me when you're available. Not urgent at all. Wren."

Wren joined Rascal and Ruby outside. "We can continue our walk while I wait for the sheriff to call."

After they circled the trailers that hadn't been totaled by the tornado, Wren's phone rang.

"You saved me from a boring meeting, Wren. What's up?" the sheriff asked.

"My publisher wants me to leave for my next assignment, but I wanted to check with you to be sure there aren't any reasons I can't leave."

"There aren't; when does he want you to leave?"

"Tomorrow."

"That's awful quick for you to get ready. When do you want to leave?"

Wren grinned. "Monday."

"Turns out I can't release you until Monday." He chuckled as he hung up.

Wren sent Charlie a text. "I can leave Monday."

He immediately replied, "Bootleggers Campground, Dearheart, Tennessee. I'll text you the address of the RV dealership in Waco."

Wren texted the information to Justin.

"Okay, Rascal, let's go."

Rascal shifted direction and picked up his speed as he headed toward Gage's house. Before they reached the house, Wren heard two short bursts of the train whistle. Wren frowned. *That has to mean something.*

"Rascal, we have to find Mr. Navarro."

Rascal led the way into the woods behind the campground to the bridge. Mr. Navarro stood on the opposite side.

"I heard the signal," Wren said.

"Train is about to move." Mr. Navarro strolled away into the woods.

"Wait, does the signal tell me to move too?" Wren asked.

When Mr. Navarro didn't respond, Wren muttered, "Why tell me something if you aren't going to tell me what it means?"

Rascal grinned at the soft, deep-voiced chuckle from the woods.

"Zuri's laughing at me, isn't she?"

Ruby yipped.

"Y'all are ganging up on me, but I get it." Wren smiled. "Are we ready to go back to the office?"

Ruby led the way back.

"Good job, Ruby." Wren opened the door to the office.

"There you are," Kendra said. "Aunt Jenna Lee may be a little late; Ralph called and said she had a plumbing emergency; he was on his way to see if it was something he could fix well enough to get her through the weekend."

Ruby trotted to her water bowl and took a long drink.

When her phone rang, Kendra shook her head. "It's Walt; he must have one of his emergencies."

She listened for a few minutes. "Okay, I'll be right there."

Kendra sighed. "One of their trucks broke down, and Walt needs me to pick him up in the golf cart, so he can get the tool they need to fix it. Of course, I'll have to take him back because he doesn't want to leave me without the golf cart, which by the way, would not be necessary if we had that utility vehicle for maintenance; at least that's what I expect him to explain in excruciating detail when I pick him up." Kendra rolled her eyes.

After Kendra left, Wren sat on the stool at the desk and checked the computer for any new registrations.

Her phone buzzed a text from Justin. "Thanks."

When Wren swung her foot around the stool to climb down, she kicked a box under the desk and frowned. *Walt found crossword puzzles in Miss Jenna Lee's safe.*

Wren pulled out the box from the shelf to the floor and opened it. *Crossword puzzle books.* When she picked up the booklet on top, loose completed crossword pages and other papers dropped out and scattered on the floor, leaving only the cover in her hand.

"What on earth?"

Rascal and Ruby investigated the paper on the floor while Wren picked up two crossword pages and several typed sheets; she set the two crossword pages on the desk then quickly scanned one of the typed pages. "This reads like part of a legal document."

As Wren picked up more of the papers and put them into page number order, Kendra returned.

"It didn't take nearly as long as I expected because Walt grabbed what they needed, then I ran him back to the worksite. They weren't that far away, but..." Kendra stared at the papers on the desk and floor. "What are those?"

"I'm not sure. Miss Jenna Lee told me they were her completed crossword puzzles, but it looks like she removed the pages and inserted the rest of these papers between the front and back cover."

Kendra read the first page. "This reads like a will, but it doesn't matter anymore, does it?"

"I wouldn't think so because she has a new will."

"Let's pick up the papers and put the box back before Aunt Jenna Lee gets here. We wouldn't want her to think we were snooping."

"Which is exactly what I was doing." Wren giggled as she handed pages to Kendra, who put the pages in between the covers.

As they put the box back in its place on the shelf under the desk, Kendra said, "One thing that bothered me when I picked up Walt is that he had a cut on his hand. It was minor, and I was going to give him a bandage to protect it from dirt, but he wouldn't let me take time to find one. I'd like to have a first aid kit in the golf cart. Maybe there are a few supplies here that I could pull together even a simple one. Would you check the drawers while I check the storeroom to see what we have."

After they completed their search and found no first aid supplies, Kendra said, "I hoped I'd at least find a small toolbox that I could repurpose for our first aid kit but didn't find a thing. It was too much to expect, wasn't it? I'll make a list of supplies then run to the gas station if you don't mind taking care of the office until Aunt Jenna Lee arrives."

While Kendra worked on her list, Wren said, "Charlie wanted me to leave today or Sunday; I talked to the sheriff, who said I could leave on Monday, which was my preference."

"I would have suggested next month, which is probably why I didn't get to vote. Where are you going?"

"Bootleggers Creek Campground in Dearheart, Tennessee."

"Deer like the animal, or dear like precious?" Kendra asked.

"Not the animal," Wren giggled. "I can't imagine bootleggers being precious, so maybe be dear like expensive."

"I like precious better." Kendra resumed writing her notes.

When Kendra completed her list, Wren said, "Why don't I go to the gas station for you? I'd planned to go to the gas station today anyway to see if they have a yellow shirt in honor of my sunflowers."

Kendra furrowed her brow. "Are you sure? Will you be okay?"

"I'll have Rascal with me."

"That's true; I'll add a small box to the list; let me know if this makes sense." Kendra handed the list to Wren, who quickly read it.

"Looks fine to me." When Wren and Rascal headed toward the door, Ruby yipped.

Wren asked, "Is it okay with you if Ruby goes with us?"

Kendra smiled. "That's fine."

Rascal ran to the pickup that was parked in front of the camper, and Ruby kept up with him. When Wren joined them, Ruby grinned.

"It was a good run, wasn't it, Ruby?"

Wren opened the back door, and Rascal hopped into the pickup. "Go ahead, Ruby; you can do it."

Ruby tentatively put her front paws on the running board then jumped inside.

After Wren parked in front of the store, she opened the back door, and Rascal and Ruby jumped out then trotted to the shade at the far side of the store near the woods.

"I won't be long." Wren went inside; after she found a small shopping cart, she read over her list then hesitated while she wondered where the first aid supplies were.

"Second aisle," Harper said.

Wren peered at her. "Are you a mind reader?"

Harper giggled. "Ms. Kendra called and said you'd be shopping for first aid supplies, and I should put everything on the campground's bill, but I like your idea better."

Wren smiled. "Thanks, so do I."

After she found all the first aid supplies on the list, Wren headed to the sporting goods section to look for a tackle box that would work as a first aid kit.

Wren frowned at the tackle boxes next to the fishing poles. "Too large," she muttered.

Wren heard two quiet, quick taps behind her, on her right; when she shifted in the direction of the taps, her friend was next to her. "What about these?" He pointed to the small tackle boxes.

"That's absolutely perfect; I wouldn't have seen them if you hadn't caught my attention."

"Move right is the right move." The man strolled away; before he turned at the end of the aisle, he said, "One down, but you have to remember one across."

"What?" Wren's eyes widened.

That sounded like something Miss Jenna Lee would say.

Wren shook off her confusion then hurried to look at the T-shirts. She wrinkled her nose at the only yellow T-shirt she found. *Too bright. I'll just keep looking.*

After Harper rang up and sacked Wren's purchases, Wren picked up the three sacks.

Harper said, "I thought you and Rascal had Ruby with you, but I looked out a few minutes ago and didn't see her, so I..."

Wren didn't hear the rest because she rushed out of the store; Rascal was alone in front of the pickup.

Wren quickly scanned the parking lot and the area alongside the woods. "Where's Ruby?"

Rascal whined.

When a yelp of pain came from somewhere beyond the trees, Rascal tore into the woods as a car skidded to a stop next to Wren's truck.

That was Ruby. Wren dropped her packages and raced after him. She quickly lost sight of Rascal; she stopped to listen for him and heard Ruby whimper in the woods to her left.

"Rascal," she shouted.

Rascal barked twice.

Before she could call out again, she heard two quick bursts of the train whistle and wheeled right and looked behind her.

Ralph was within twenty feet of her. He held a bloody baseball bat in his right hand but dropped it. Wren put her hands on her waist with her right hand ready to draw.

Ralph snarled. "You've been nothing but trouble for me. Too bad old Jenna Lee had that terrible accident in the tub, then you were savagely attacked in the woods when one of your dogs ran away from you."

"What about Raleigh Baker and Nelson Decker?" Wren asked. "Did they have terrible accidents too?"

Ralph spit on the ground. "Baker got greedy. He said he was doing all the dirty work and wanted a bigger cut." Ralph's laugh was cruel and hollow. "I gave him exactly what he asked for. Nelson Decker was a fool. He said he was tired and wanted out; I was happy to oblige him."

"Not so fast, Carson," the deputy appeared in the woods on Ralph's left. "Put up your hands."

When Ralph shifted his attention to the deputy, who had his gun drawn, Wren took a few steps farther left to widen the angle between her and the deputy.

Ralph turned his head toward Wren when she moved and pulled out his pistol.

"Drop it, Ralph," the deputy growled.

Ralph swung left and fired at the deputy; Wren drew her pistol and shot Ralph.

Wren called nine-one-one.

"Wren, the deputy will be..."

Wren interrupted her. "Ralph Carson shot the deputy in the shoulder; I shot Ralph; his breathing is a little ragged and shallow. I have to find Rascal and Ruby, then we'll meet the sheriff in the parking lot."

Rascal and Ruby barked, and Wren hurried toward them. When she reached them, Ruby was tied to a tree. She kept her left paw raised.

Wren froze. "Miss Jenna Lee."

She pulled out her phone and called the campground.

"Kendra, I think Miss Jenna Lee is badly hurt in her bathroom. Can you send Walt to her house as fast as he can get there?"

"Will do. We'll talk later." Kendra hung up.

Wren removed the rope from around Ruby's neck then gently examined her paw. Ruby whined.

"I'm sorry, girl. Can you stay here while we get help?"

Ruby slowly laid down on the dried pine needles.

"I'm going to check the deputy, Rascal, then we'll need to meet the sheriff."

Rascal joined Ruby on the pine needles.

Wren nodded. "I'll be back with help as soon as I can."

When Wren reached the deputy, he was on his knees; he clutched his bleeding shoulder and tried to rise.

Wren helped him up. "Lean on me."

"You can't hold me up, Wren."

"I'm stronger than I look; let's go."

Chapter Sixteen

On the way to the parking lot, the deputy said, "You're a good shot."

"Thanks to my dad," Wren said. "How did you know we needed help?"

"Harper called the dispatcher and said that someone must have taken Ruby from the gas station; I heard Rascal barking, so I was trying to find him. I can't tell you how shocked I was when I saw Ralph and heard what he said about Baker and Decker; I even hesitated for a second to draw on him."

"I didn't think so."

"Thanks; the sheriff told me about the marshal in Arizona; he's a lucky guy, but does he have any idea of what he's getting into?" The deputy chuckled then tried to stifle a cough.

He groaned, "That was a mistake."

"I don't know your name, Deputy."

"Sean. Where do you go from here?" He stumbled on a tree root.

Wren grunted as she held onto him and widened her stance to brace herself while she kept him from falling.

"Tennessee; do you need a break? We can stop for a second."

"No, let's keep going unless you need a break," Sean said.

"We've got momentum on our side, so let's keep moving." She gritted her teeth. *Before I wear out.*

"When do you leave?" Sean asked.

"Monday."

"So soon? You'll always have friends in Dry Creek, you know."

Wren nodded. "It's hard to leave good friends."

Before they cleared the trees, the sheriff shouted, "Wren!"

"Here; we're right here," she called out.

When the sheriff reached them, he said, "I'll take over, Wren. Where are Rascal and Ruby?"

The sheriff supported Sean as the three of them continued through the trees to the parking lot.

"Rascal stayed with Ruby. Ralph Carson hurt Ruby's paw, so she would cry out."

As they continued toward the parking lot, the sheriff said, "Walt called me; Miss Jenna Lee is on the way to the hospital; she has a broken arm and a goose egg over her eye. She told Walt she threw up her arms to protect her head, then when she saw the blood, she fell over and held her breath. I guess she's on a blood thinner because Walt said there was blood everywhere. She is one feisty old lady, but don't tell her I said she was old," the sheriff said. "Wren, can you lead the ambulance crew to Ralph? I'll get someone to go along with us to help me with Ruby."

When they reached the parking lot, one ambulance crew rushed to Sean with their cot while the second crew removed their cot from the back of the ambulance.

Gage jumped out of his car, rushed to Wren, and put his arm around her. "I'm your cousin too; are you okay?"

The sheriff's mouth twitched. "I have myself a volunteer, don't I, Wren?"

"Volunteer for what?" Gage asked.

"Ruby's hurt; she'll have to be carried out," the sheriff said.

"I have a quilt in my truck; she'll be more comfortable with a makeshift litter. I'll take her to the vet," Gage said.

"Where's our patient, Sheriff?" the paramedic asked.

After Gage returned with the quilt, the sheriff said, "Follow us."

On the way to the woods, Gage said, "Wren, Mom picked up the puppies; they're with her at the office. Mom said I couldn't tell you anything because she wants to tell you herself, which is fair enough because I don't know much at all. Mom called me and told me to show up at the gas station to help you."

After the ambulance crew reached Ralph, the paramedic said, "Still breathing; let's get him to the ambulance."

"This way for Ruby," Wren said.

Rascal yipped when Wren, Gage, and the sheriff arrived.

Gage gently lifted Ruby to the quilt, then he and the sheriff grabbed the ends and carried Ruby in her makeshift hammock to Gage's truck while Rascal trotted alongside her; Wren followed them.

Rascal whined after Gage and the sheriff put Ruby on the backseat.

"Gage will bring Ruby to Kendra's house after the vet treats her, won't you, Gage?" Wren asked.

"You can count on it. See you later."

After Gage left, the sheriff said, "Wren, tell me what happened; I'll get the official version from my deputy."

Sheriff took notes while Wren told him about trying to find Rascal and Ruby, then Carson and his attempted ambush and what he said about Miss Jenna Lee.

"Why did you call Kendra to have Walt check on Jenna Lee?"

"I knew Walt could get there faster than anyone else because the campground is so close to her house; if what Ralph told me was true, I didn't think she had much time."

"It was a gutsy call, but I'd have done the same thing under the circumstances. My deputy will provide his report for our records. Are you still planning to leave on Monday? We'll all miss you. When you talk to your marshal, tell him to call me, and I'll give him a full report."

"Thanks; I think he'll appreciate it."

After Wren and Rascal were in the pickup, Wren glanced toward the store. Her friend stood at attention near the door. As she pulled away, he saluted her. Wren put her hand on her heart then smiled as she waved good-bye.

As she headed toward the campground, Wren said, "This is another anytime, isn't it? I need to call Justin."

After she parked in front of her camper, she and Rascal went inside. Wren poured a glass of sweet tea then called Justin.

"Perfect timing, honey. I'm doing paperwork. What's your day like?"

"Do you want the short version or the long version?"

"Short," he said.

"I shot the bad guy after he shot the deputy, and the sheriff said for you to call him, and he'll give you a full report."

"What? I did say short, didn't I? Are you and Rascal okay?"

"We're fine; we're at the camper, and we're safe."

"Are there any more bad guys?"

"No, the man I shot killed his two partners."

Wren bit her lip then continued, "I wanted you to know that your dream made a difference because the bad guy set up an ambush by hurting a dog, and Rascal ran to see why she yelped with pain. I knew somebody was going to ambush me because of your dream; I just didn't know who."

"Who was it?"

"The man who gave Miss Jenna Lee the puppies."

"He had the mama dog, didn't he? Is that who he hurt?"

"Yes, it was. The man was going to put her down yesterday, but Walt intervened and took her home. Walt called her Ruby, and she liked it."

"Ruby didn't have a name?"

"I think he called her the mama dog."

"I'm glad you shot him, honey. You sure you're safe?"

"Yes; we'll stay with Kendra and Walt again tonight."

"Good, I'll call you later; is that okay?" Justin asked.

"That would be great."

After they hung up, Wren stared at the phone. *Only two more campgrounds to go.*

"Let's go see Kendra, Rascal. I think she has the puppies."

Rascal grinned when Wren opened the front door then bounded to the office.

When they went inside, Coco and Luna yipped then pranced to Rascal. Wren opened the door, and the three of them raced outside.

"Our girls are going to miss Rascal; he'll be like their favorite teacher that they'll always remember."

"Did you go through the papers that were between the crossword puzzle covers?" Wren asked.

"Did I ever! Gage will take them to Aunt Jenna Lee's lawyer in Waco on Monday for an official review, but you would not believe what I found."

Wren rolled her eyes. "I might."

Kendra smiled. "Aunt Jenna Lee had the original deed and the contract for the property that the speculator bought from the Navarro families. The speculator sold the property, the complete parcel, back to the Navarro family that owned the zoo and train station property. Aunt Jenna Lee had that contract and the title for all the property."

"What about the campground? Didn't someone else own it? This isn't what Miss Jenna Lee told me at all. All this is so like her, isn't it?" Wren shook her head.

"He was leasing it from Aunt Jenna Lee. Here's the kicker: Walt and Gage bought the property from Aunt Jenna Lee."

"So, I'm still not sure why she was so secretive about owning all the property, unless she was afraid that someone would take it away from her, but who could that be? She thought Eric Decker was helping her hang onto the property, except he and the accountant were robbing her by skimming off the top, weren't they?" Wren asked.

"That's what Tara thinks from the papers she has. Ralph was part of Aunt Jenna Lee's inner circle because she and his wife were so close. Some people said that he blamed Aunt Jenna Lee for his wife's suicide, but some people are nosy busybodies who like to stir up trouble."

Wren nodded. "I have been here less than a week, but I know exactly who you're talking about."

"I'm not really surprised; those two stalk the aisles at the gas station for snippets of conversations they can turn into gossip, and if they don't hear anything, they make it up."

"What about the will?"

"I left the best for last because I think it is actually the answer to why Aunt Jenna Lee was so secretive. She had an older will that left everything to Walt's father and Walt."

"Fifteen years ago, Eric Decker wrote a will that replaced that old will; after his death, Nelson Decker revised it. The will named Ralph, George, and Nelson as her beneficiaries with rights of survivorship for each man included. I'd love to know the story of how Aunt Jenna Lee found out about the will change and obtained a copy of it, but I have a feeling Ralph's wife, who was her close friend, had a hand in that. The two of them must have decided it would be safer for Aunt Jenna Lee if no one had an inkling of what she knew. I'm going to talk to the sheriff because I'm convinced that Ralph's wife did not die by suicide. I personally think Ralph also hastened the early demise of George, Aunt Jenna Lee's accountant, and with Nelson out of the way, that left only Aunt Jenna Lee and you."

"Why me? I don't get it."

"You were a target of our gossipmongers. They claimed you were not a journalist; instead, you were an undercover cop here to expose a conspiracy. They didn't say what kind of conspiracy, but Ralph must have believed the gossip and was certain you were about to expose him."

"What a tangled mess," Wren said.

Kendra nodded. "The new will helps tremendously; I hope Tara stays on as the accountant for the campground because the records definitely need work. I'm a little worried about the taxes, but I can't see where George would have wanted to trigger a tax audit, so they might be fine. So, you're all caught up on the Navarro story; now tell me what your plans are."

"I'll pack tomorrow then leave early Monday morning. I'll pick up a new camper in Waco, then we'll head east for Tennessee."

"You're staying with us tonight, right? Bring any laundry, so you'll be completely caught up. I plan to leave here around three," Kendra said.

"We'll follow you; I have a few things to take care of before we leave. Are you staying here, Rascal?"

Rascal glanced at the puppies then trotted to the door.

"We'll see y'all later," Wren said.

After they left, Wren said, "Let's see if we can find Mr. Navarro; we'll tell Humberto tomorrow that we're leaving early Monday morning."

As they strolled toward the woods, Wren's phone rang.

She smiled as she answered. "You must be a mind reader, Marshal."

Justin cleared his throat. "I looked up the route to Dearheart, Tennessee, and it's too dangerous for you to drive."

Wren narrowed her eyes. *Is he saying I'm an incompetent driver?* "Oh, really?"

"Yes," he continued. "There's no way to get there by interstate; the roads are narrow with hairpin curves. It would be hard for you to drive your truck safely, but it's out of the question with you pulling a trailer."

Wren gritted her teeth. "Anything else?"

Justin exhaled. "No, that's it; I just had to make sure we were clear that it's not safe for you to go."

"I have things to do." Wren's voice was cold.

"I'm busy too."

Wren hung up. "Justin has crossed a line, Rascal. He essentially said I'm not a competent driver, but I am not going to let him ruin my day."

As they continued through the woods toward the bridge, Wren smiled at the sound of a child who giggled in the woods. Their arrival at the bridge was announced by one long blast of the train whistle; Señor Navarro waited for them in the middle of the bridge.

"The train is approaching the station; we appreciate your help, Wren Weaver, in clearing the way for the Navarro family to be back in business."

Zuri roared with delight from the trees.

"We're all grateful." Señor Navarro bowed then disappeared.

As Wren and Rascal headed back to their camper to prepare for their next adventure, the little girl laughed, Zuri roared, and the steam whistle blasted long and loud.

Chapter Seventeen

While Wren brushed her teeth before bed that night, she gazed at her phone that was on the counter near the sink and sighed. *Justin's not going to call. He thinks he won, and I'm not going to Tennessee.*

After she changed into pajamas, she rubbed Rascal's face and hugged him; she was startled when her phone buzzed.

She snatched up her phone. "It's Justin, Rascal."

Her mouth twitched into a wicked smile as she read the text. "I'm so sorry I'm a knucklehead."

Wren replied, "I am too."

When she answered her phone on the first ring, Justin was laughing. "I understood exactly what you were saying, honey. You win; I love you."

Wren's eyes widened. "Say it again."

The tone of his voice became serious. "I love you, Wren."

She smiled. "I love you too."

Next to read:

MURDER IN THE MOUNTAINS

WREN AND RASCAL COZY MYSTERY, BOOK 3

Wren and Rascal leave Arizona for her second writing assignment: a haunted campground in Texas. A killer wants her dead.

Wren and Rascal, her protective, mostly Labrador Retriever, discover a dead man in the woods. It's obvious who the killer is, isn't it? Even the ghost tells her not everyone is who they seem.

Check BARRETT BOOK SHOP to find your next book to read!

Browse, shop, read, enjoy!

Acknowledgements

Huge thanks to my husband for his patience, support, talented technical expertise, and guidance.

Thanks to my editor, family, friends, and faithful readers for their awesome support and encouragement.

Thank you for reading. You keep reading; I'll keep writing!

Tell a friend how much you love Wren and Rascal and a leave a short review with Barrett Book Shop or your favorite retailer. Authors can always use a few sparkles to brighten the gloomiest days.

PRO TIP: Post a five-star rating or recommend a book: both count the same as reviews!

Ready for news about what's next? Look for the NEWSLETTER tab on JUDITHABARRETT.COM to subscribe to my not-your-typical newsletter for stories, new releases, and VIP Reader bargains!

About the Author

Judith A. Barrett, award-winning author, lives on a farm in Georgia with her husband, two dogs, and chickens. She writes series for her readers: thriller, mystery, post-apocalyptic science fiction, and cozy mystery novels. Stories with a twist: not your typical characters from not your typical author!

When she isn't writing, Judith is working on farm chores, hiking or camping with her husband and dogs, or rocking on her front porch while she watches the sunset.

You keep reading; I'll keep writing!

website: www.judithabarrett.com

BARRETT BOOK SHOP

Browse, shop, read, enjoy!

BarrettBookShop.com

Subscribe to her enewsletter via her website

Let's keep in touch!